The Case of the Unfettered Utonagan

A Thousand Islands Doggy Inn Mystery

B.R. Snow

Copyright © 2018 B.R. Snow

ISBN: 978-1-942691-58-7

Website: www.brsnow.net/

Twitter: @BernSnow

Facebook: facebook.com/bernsnow

Cover Design: Reggie Cullen

Cover Photo: James R. Miller

Other Books by B.R. Snow

The Thousand Islands Doggy Inn Mysteries

- The Case of the Abandoned Aussie
- The Case of the Brokenhearted Bulldog
- The Case of the Caged Cockers
- The Case of the Dapper Dandie Dinmont
- The Case of the Eccentric Elkhound
- The Case of the Faithful Frenchie
- The Case of the Graceful Goldens
- The Case of the Hurricane Hounds
- The Case of the Itinerant Ibizan
- The Case of the Jaded Jack Russell
- The Case of the Klutz King Charles
- The Case of the Lovable Labs
- The Case of the Mellow Maltese
- The Case of the Natty Newfie
- The Case of the Overdue Otterhound
- The Case of the Prescient Poodle
- The Case of the Quizzical Queens Beagle
- The Case of the Reliable Russian Spaniels
- The Case of the Salubrious Soft Coated Wheaten
- The Case of Italian Indigestion (A Josie and Chef Claire Sojourn)
- The Case of the Tenacious Tibetan

The Whiskey Run Chronicles

- The Whiskey Run Chronicles – The Complete Volume 1
- The Whiskey Run Chronicles – The Complete Volume 2

The Damaged Posse

- American Midnight
- Larrikin Gene
- Sneaker World
- Summerman
- The Duplicates

Other Books

- Divorce Hotel
- Either Ore

To all my readers

You're the best!

Chapter 1

I pushed myself up out of my chair and took baby steps across the office to adjust the thermostat. I turned the heat up then glanced out the window. Several dogs were wrestling and rolling around in the fresh snow that had fallen yesterday. I shivered at the thought of being outside, but the dogs either didn't realize how cold it was or didn't care. I leaned forward to pet all four house dogs who were sprawled out on the couch. Al and Dente, Chef Claire's Golden Retrievers, were nestled close to each other and sound asleep. But when I scratched Al's ears, he opened one eye, thumped his tail on the couch then drifted off. Chloe, my Aussie shepherd, was tucked up against Captain. The massive Newfie was snoring and dominating most of the couch.

"You sure you guys wouldn't like to go out and play in the snow?"

Chloe looked up and snorted as if asking me if I was out of my mind. She stretched her front and back legs to the max then closed her eyes and tucked herself even closer to Captain's chest.

"Tough life you guys lead, huh?" I said with a grin as I sat back down at the desk.

I rummaged through the drawers for something to eat but came up empty. I glanced at the small stack of paperwork and decided it could wait. My eyes landed on an Agatha Christie book I was halfway through. I was convinced I knew who the murderer was but kept reading since Agatha usually had something up her sleeve. I got through another chapter before the knock.

"Come in," I said as I dog-eared the page and slid the book to one side.

Sammy entered, trailed by Dr. Lacey Adams. They both reacted to the temperature in the office and removed their coats. The dogs stirred, but apart from some tail thumps, stayed right where they were.

"Hey, guys," I said, gesturing for them to take a seat. "You finished already?"

"Yeah," Sammy said, remaining on his feet. "We didn't dawdle while we were out there."

"You got that right," Lacey said with a chuckle.

"We toured as much of the shelter as we could," he said. "But the drifts are pretty high in a couple of spots."

"Thanks, Sammy," I said. "Appreciate you taking the time. I would have done it, but...well, you know," I said, patting my enormous stomach.

"No problem. I'll leave you two alone," Sammy said. "I've got some things to take care of."

"Thanks, Sammy," I said. "I'll see you before I head up to the house."

He departed with a wave and gently closed the door behind him.

"He's good," Lacey said.

"Yeah, we're really lucky to have him. Jill, too," I said, then shrugged. "In fact, all of our folks are great."

"How many staff do you have?"

"Let's see," I said, doing the math. "Counting part-timers, we're up to a dozen."

"Nice," she said. "You said there are three assigned to the rescue shelter, right?"

"Yeah. But a lot of the folks who work with the dogs help out down there when needed. And if the thing keeps growing, we're going to need more."

"Hence, the decision to hire another vet, right?"

"Not just another vet," I said with a smile. "We're hiring you."

Lacey beamed at me.

"Can I ask how many people applied for the job?"

"Geez, we had a bunch," I said. "But a lot of them didn't have experience with large animals."

"I still can't believe you have an elephant," she said. "There has to be a story behind that."

"Yeah. The circus came to town but left in pieces. Beulah needed a home, so we took her in."

"She seems to be doing well."

"Much better than she was with the circus."

"I know I should have asked already, but how the heck did you end up with an animal shelter?"

"My mother owned all the acreage behind the Inn and couldn't decide what she wanted to do with it. So, we eventually came up with the idea. It's taken some time for it to grow, but the word has gotten out, and we're getting all sorts of requests to take animals in."

"You have to be losing your shirt on it," Lacey said.

"You worried it might not make it?"

"Well, yeah. A little," she said, forcing a smile.

"You don't have to worry. The shelter's set up as a non-profit, and my mother heads the board of directors. She has a lot of rich friends and isn't shy about hitting them up for donations. The interest on the endowment covers the operating expenses."

"That's good to know. Your mom must be a whizz at fundraising."

"Well, she doesn't take no for an answer easily. Trust me on that one."

"I can't wait to meet her," Lacey said. "Where's Josie?"

"She and Chef Claire went cross-country skiing." I patted my belly and grinned at her. "Fortunately, I have a good excuse for not participating in that particular form of torture."

"Yeah, it's never been my favorite either," she said. "I prefer downhill. You know, let the mountain do all the work for me."

"Smart," I said, nodding. "Do you have any more questions before you sign the contract?"

"Just a few details. When would you like me to start?"

"As soon as possible," I said. "Josie's been doing everything by herself, and it's just too much."

"No problem. I'm ready to start anytime," Lacey said. "But I need to find a place to live."

"I think we can help you with that. Our friend Rooster has a rental that's vacant at the moment."

"Rooster?"

"Yeah. You're gonna like him. He's as unique as his name. The house is only a two-bedroom, but it's just you, right?"

"It is," she said, frowning. "I'm still between relationships."

"How long has it been?"

"Over two years," Lacey said. "After we broke up, I decided I needed a long break."

"I'm sorry to hear that. What happened?"

"Early on, I made one big mistake," she said, shrugging.

"Only one? That's not bad. What was it?"

"I believed him when he said he was going to leave his wife."

"Oh," I said with a frown.

"Yeah, the familiar, yet tragic, tale of a grad student falling for a professor," she said. "I'm such a cliché."

"One of your professors?"

"No, he was an adjunct professor at Copeland College while I was a vet student at Cornell. But he's not there anymore. He and the Copeland administrators came to an understanding."

"It sounds like there's more to the story."

"I'm sure there is," she said. "But Jeremy wasn't willing to share it. It's pretty clear there was a lot of bad blood on both sides."

"When did he leave the university?" I said, doing my best to get comfortable in my chair.

"It's been awhile. I'd already graduated. And we were done by then," she said, drifting off for a moment. "I met Jeremy when he was presenting his latest research at a faculty symposium. Soon after we met, I started working for him on a part-time basis."

"I don't remember discussing that during the interview," I said, searching my memory bank.

"No, you guys spent most of the time asking about my internship in Africa."

"It was fascinating. Working with elephants and lions. What an experience."

"It was incredible."

"What's his research focused on?" I said.

"Wolves. Anyway, we started seeing each other, and it took off in a hurry. But soon, it was all downhill."

"Like skiing?"

"Exactly. A black diamond run."

I chuckled and grabbed her contract from a drawer and slid it across the desk.

"Here you go. Take all the time you need to look it over."

"Is it pretty much what we discussed during the interview?" Lacey said.

"It is," I said, rubbing my stomach. "Oh, I did add one job duty. I put something in about covering here at the Inn from time to time when Josie's away. Or when we're in Cayman during the winter."

"That's fine," she said, flipping to the last page. "We talked about that."

"But don't be shy about taking a vacation," I said. "Josie's happy to cover for you. And if you both need to be away at the same time, we'll find coverage."

"Okay, let's do this," she said, signing the contract and sliding it back to me.

"Great," I said, beaming at her. "Welcome aboard."

"Thanks, Suzy. I've been looking for something like this since I finished school."

"We're glad we found you, Lacey," I said, extending my hand. "A bunch of us are having dinner at the restaurant tonight. And Rooster will be there. He said he's happy to discuss the house and give you a tour. And my mom will be there."

"Sounds good. What time?"

"Around seven," I said. "We usually meet in the lounge for a drink first."

"I'll be there," she said, getting to her feet. "And I'd like to start tomorrow if that's okay."

"Perfect." My phone chirped. "Hang on just a sec. It's Josie." I put the phone on speaker and set it down on the desk. "Hey, how's it going out there?"

"Chef Claire is a maniac," Josie said. "I'm not going to be able to walk for a week."

"It's good for you. It builds character," I said, laughing. "You called just to complain?"

"No, actually we need you to get a condo ready," Josie said. "We're bringing a new guest in."

"You found a stray out there?"

"I'm not exactly sure what we've got. But she's definitely on her own at the moment."

"What kind of dog is it?"

"I think I'll wait and surprise you."

"Okay, you've got my attention. Where are you?"

"We're about ten minutes out."

"Is the dog okay?"

"She's fine. But I will want to check her out. Could you have one of the folks get an exam room ready? And she's going to need some food and a big bowl of water."

"You got it," I said.

"Oh, make sure the house dogs are in your office, and all the other dogs are in their condos. Just to be on the safe side."

"What the heck are you bringing in? Bigfoot?"

"Funny. Okay, I gotta run."

"See you when you get here."

I ended the call and frowned.

"The poor thing," I said to Lacey. "What's a stray doing out in the woods in February?"

"It happens, right?" she said.

"Yeah. But it's pretty remote where they went skiing. The dog has to be a long way from home."

"You mind if I stick around until they get here?"

"I'd be surprised if you didn't," I said, grinning at her.

Chapter 2

Chef Claire held the front door open as Josie led our new guest inside. The dog wasn't happy being tethered to a lead, but tentatively walked into the registration area and surveyed the room. She was big, about eighty pounds, and had beautiful white and grey fur accented with black. Her green eyes pierced the air as she continued to take in her surroundings. I approached and tentatively extended a hand. The dog sniffed it then resumed her surveillance.

"Is that what I think it is?" I said, glancing at Josie.

"To tell you the truth," she said, sitting down. "I'm not exactly sure."

"I don't believe it," Lacey said, slowly approaching the dog. "Akna?"

The dog cocked her head at our new vet then sniffed and licked her hand. It sat down on its haunches and stared up at her.

"Akna?" Josie said. The dog looked at Josie expectantly. "You know the dog?"

"I think I do," Lacey said, still stunned. "I recognize that white streak crisscrossing down her chest. Akna is an Alaskan name for goddess."

"This is weird," Chef Claire said. "She's not a wolf, is she?"

"No," Lacey said. "Well, maybe a little."

"I think we're going to need a bit more, Lacey," Josie said.

"She's a Utonagan," Lacey said, rubbing the dog's ears.

"How did you pronounce that?" Chef Claire said.

"You-ton-are-gan," Lacey said, enunciating each syllable. "It means the spirit of the wolf."

"I remember," Josie said, nodding. "The breed was created in England, right?"

"Yes," Lacey said. "The Utonagan was originally created by breeding Huskies, German Shepherds, and Malamutes with different mixed-breed dogs."

"Dogs as a science experiment?" Chef Claire said, frowning.

"Yes, I'm afraid so," Lacey said. "A lot of the breeding practices have been controversial. The original idea was to create a dog that looked like a wolf but had the gentle nature of a domesticated dog."

"Well, this one isn't what I'd call domesticated," Josie said. "At least, not completely."

"I think Akna might have some percentage of wolf in her," Lacey said. "I'm not sure how much. I can't believe it's her. She was just a pup the last time I saw her."

"Okay, I gotta ask," I said, staring at Lacey. "How the heck do you know the dog?"

"Because of Dr. Jeremy Peters," she said.

"Why does that name sound familiar?" I said, searching my memory bank.

"You're probably thinking of Peters' Hybrid Consortium," Lacey said.

"From your resume," Josie said. "You worked there for a while."

"I did. He's a famous researcher."

"Your ex-boyfriend?" I said.

"Yeah, that's him," Lacey said. "He's one of the leading experts in grey wolves."

"No, that's not where I know his name from," I said, concentrating hard.

Sammy entered the registration area and stopped dead in his tracks when he saw the dog.

"Where the heck did you find her?" he said, slowly approaching the Utonagan.

"Near Sebastian Pines," Chef Claire said.

"I was about to get her dinner ready, but thought I should check to see what you want to use."

"Let's go with the high protein, large dog formula," Josie said. "And a big bowl of water."

"You got it," he said, heading back into the condo area.

Josie stroked the dog's back and gently probed her ribs.

"She's a little emaciated. Probably hasn't eaten for a few days," she said, studying the dog closely. "What the heck was she doing out in the middle of the woods?"

"Probably looking for Suka," Lacey said, then caught the looks we were giving her. "Suka is her mate. Or at least that was Jeremy's plan at the time when Akna was a pup."

"Is this Suka a wolf?" I said.

"He's not a purebred, but he's close," Lacey said.

Sammy returned with the food and water and set both bowls down in front of the dog. Akna sniffed the food then devoured it. When she finished, she turned her attention to the water and drank for a long time.

"So, what exactly is this Dr. Peters up to?" Josie said.

"He wants to reintroduce the grey wolf to the native environment. They're pretty much extinct around here, but his goal is to come up with a protected hybrid breed that can survive on its own, but not be a threat to people."

"Geez," Josie said, shaking her head. "Why can't people just leave the natural order alone?"

"Jeremy believes wolves are an integral component of the ecosystem," Lacey said.

"But if he's successful, he wouldn't be reintroducing the wolf," Josie said.

"No, he wouldn't," Lacey said. "And he and I had many conversations about that very subject. But Jeremy is determined to do something about the situation. And very devoted to his research. Not to mention quite eccentric."

"He sounds like a nutjob," Josie said.

"You're not the first person to call him that," Lacey said.

"Why does his name sound familiar?" I said. "It's driving me crazy."

"Just let it marinate," Josie said. "So, what do we do with her?"

"Well, I'd rather not have to talk to him," Lacey said as she reached for her phone. "But let me give him a call." She scrolled through her contacts then made the call. She caught the look I was giving her and shrugged. "I haven't gotten around to deleting his number." She continued to hold the phone to her ear then put it away. "It just kept ringing. And he refuses to set up his voice mail. Says if people really want to speak with him, they'll keep trying. I'll call him again in a bit."

"We'll just keep her here for the night," I said. "Do you know how she is around other dogs?"

"I think you need to be careful," Lacey said. "She seems to be okay with people, but I think she might have enough preying instincts to be dangerous around your dogs. Especially the smaller breeds."

"Okay," I said with a shrug. "We'll use our isolation strategy."

"Yeah, definitely," Josie said. "She probably needs to take care of business before we put her in her condo. Are all the dogs inside?"

"Yeah," Sammy said. "I got them in early because of the cold."

"Let's do this," Josie said, getting to her feet. "Okay, Akna, you ready to go out?"

We all followed Josie as she led the Utonagan to the condo area. The dog stopped in her tracks when she noticed the other dogs and hunched down as she looked up and down the rows of condos. A soft, low guttural growl emerged from somewhere deep inside.

"Good call on the isolation," Josie said, gently pulling the lead toward the door.

"Yeah," I said, nodding. "She's gonna be a handful."

"Hopefully, it's just for one night," Josie said. "Chef Claire, can you get the door?"

She pulled the door open and stepped back to give Josie and the dog room. We all stepped outside into the cold and watched as Josie removed the lead. The dog took a few tentative steps out onto the two-acre play area then got more comfortable. Akna stalked the perimeter of the seven-foot fence surrounding the area, apparently searching for an escape route.

"That tree stump is so ugly," Josie said, staring at the snow-covered object at the far end of the play area.

"Yes, it certainly is," I said.

The stump in question was all that was left of a large tree we'd had to remove in the fall. The root system had begun to work its way under the fence, and a local arborist had recommended its removal before it did any real damage. But we'd been hit with an early winter, and the ground had frozen before the arborist had time to remove the stump and roots. As such, we were now waiting impatiently for spring to arrive so we could remove the eyesore.

"Does your boyfriend realize what he's done?" Josie said to Lacey.

"Ex-boyfriend. What do you mean?"

"His goal was to create the best of both worlds," Josie said. "But it appears he might have come up with the worst of both."

"A dog that can't survive in the wild, but can't be trusted being around people?" I said.

"You got it," Josie said. "The poor animal. She might end up in limbo."

"Sadly, Jeremy is only focused on the end result," Lacey said. "And if it takes him several generations to get there, it's just one of the byproducts of scientific experiment."

"And if he ruins dozens of dogs' lives in the process, so be it?" Josie said, shaking her head in disgust.

"That's Jeremy," Lacey said. "Higher purpose and all that."

"I'd so love to have a little chat with this guy," Josie said.

"Me too," I said, studying the dog that had worked her way to the far end of the play area.

The dog came to a stop directly in front of the tree stump and squatted in the snow. She finished taking care of business then began slowly walking back toward us.

"At least she's smart enough to come in out of the cold," Josie said, watching the dog's approach.

Then the dog stopped and turned around. The Utonagan began sprinting through the snow, then jumped up on the tree stump and launched herself through the air. Her front legs reached the top of the fence, and the dog pulled herself up. She paused on top, glanced back at us then disappeared from sight.

"Holy crap," I whispered, stunned by what I'd just witnessed.

"Wow," Josie said. "How the heck did she do that?"

"Smart dog," Lacey said. "And strong. Jeremy always said one of his goals was to produce *unfettered* hybrids."

"Mission accomplished," Josie said.

"What do we do now?" Chef Claire said.

"We have to go find her," I said with a shrug.

"Tonight? In the dark?" Josie said.

"No, we'll have to wait until morning," I said. "What are the chances she'll go back to where they found her today?"

"I imagine they're pretty good," Lacey said. "Especially if she's looking for Suka."

"Have you met the male?" Josie said.

"Only from a distance. He was still a pup when I left and very skittish. It was clear from the start he didn't like people."

"Well, at least we'll get another day of cross-country in," Chef Claire said, smiling at Josie.

"You are so weird," Josie said, heading back inside.

Chapter 3

I removed my coat and handed it to the hostess then waited for Josie to do the same. We walked to the lounge entrance and looked around the half-filled room. My mother hopped off her stool and beamed at me as she made the short walk. She gave Josie a quick hug and kiss then pulled me in close for an extended embrace.

"My arms aren't long enough," she said, patting my enormous belly.

"Funny, Mom. How are you doing?"

"Wonderful, darling." She looked at Josie who was grimacing and massaging her back. "What's the matter, dear?"

"I went cross-country skiing with Chef Claire."

"Brutal," she said, laughing. "But like I always say, nothing improves a cold winter day like a ten-mile trek through snowy woods. Did you close your deal with the new vet?"

"We did," I said. "She signed the contract this afternoon. She'll be joining us for dinner."

The front door opened and Rooster and Chief Abrams entered. They stomped the snow off their boots as they removed their coats.

"Evening, ladies," Rooster said.

"Hey, Rooster. Chief," I said. "Did you guys go ice fishing today?"

"We did. I'm still thawing out. Where's Paulie? I need to have a word with him."

"He went to Montreal with a couple of his buddies," my mother said.

"Business trip?" Rooster said as he gave Josie a hug.

"Hockey game," my mother said, then waved to the hostess. "I think we're ready, Julie. We're still waiting for three more, but we'll sit down while we wait."

"You got it, Mrs. C," she said, grabbing a stack of menus.

We followed her into the dining room and sat down near the fire. Moments later, Freddie, our local medical examiner, and Jackson, our former chief of police, approached and took their seats.

"Good evening, folks," Freddie said, spreading his napkin across his lap.

"Hey, Freddie," I said. "Did you catch anything today?"

"No," he snapped.

The other men laughed and grinned at each other.

"You should have stayed home and folded paper," the Chief said.

"Excuse me?" my mother said, confused by the comment.

"Freddie's latest winter self-improvement project," I said. "Origami."

"Really?" my mother said, raising an eyebrow. "Freddie, if you're looking for something to fold, I have a load of wash that just came out of the dryer."

"You're worse than him, Mrs. C.," Freddie said, nodding at the Chief.

Dr. Lacey Adams poked her head into the dining room and glanced around. I caught her eye and waved her over. She smiled at everyone then sat down next to Freddie. I handled introductions then sat back when our server approached and took our drink orders. Freddie, on point after he got his first look at Lacey, sat up straight in his chair.

"This is a beautiful restaurant," Lacey said, glancing around.

"Thanks," my mother said. "We like it. Congratulations on your new job. We're delighted to have you."

"Thank you," Lacey said. "If every day is like this afternoon, it's certainly going to be memorable."

My mother frowned then looked at me for clarification. I began recounting the highlights of our encounter with the Utonagan.

"You found the dog while you were skiing?" my mother said to Josie.

"We did," Josie said, heaping a pile of roasted red peppers on top of a piece of bread.

"The dog was in Sebastian Pines?" Rooster said, surprised. "That's a long way from anywhere."

"That's what we thought," Josie said, then took a big bite.

"I've got a question," Jackson said. "What the heck is a Utonagan?"

"It's a breed created to look like a wolf but have the personality of a domesticated dog," Josie said.

"I assume you have her at the Inn," my mother said.

"We did," I said, dredging a piece of bread in olive oil. "Until she jumped the fence."

"She went over a seven-foot fence?" Rooster said.

"She did," Josie said, nodding.

"I gotta meet this dog," he said, shaking his head.

"Well, we're heading back out tomorrow to see if we can catch her again," Josie said. "You're welcome to join us."

"This must be a rare breed, right?" Jackson said.

"Very much so," Lacey said. "But Jeremy has always loved dealing with rare things."

"Jeremy?" my mother said.

"Dr. Jeremy Peters," Lacey said. "I used to…work for him."

My mother and Rooster stared at each other, dumbfounded.

"Peters?" Rooster said. "I thought that charlatan packed up and headed west years ago."

"Me too," my mother said, then focused on Lacey.

The penny dropped.

"That's where I've heard his name. It was driving me nuts."

"How did you get involved with him?" my mother said.

"Let's say I believed him when he told me what a rare creature I was and leave it at that," Lacey said with a shrug.

"Where is he?" Rooster said.

"I don't have a clue," Lacey said. "I met him when he was an adjunct professor at Copeland College."

"How long was he there?" Rooster said.

"It must have been three or four years."

"I don't believe it," my mother said.

"Ooh, I sense a story about to unfold," Josie said, reaching for her wine glass.

"Me too," I said, leaning forward as I focused on my mother. "I remember the name, but you always refused to go into the details."

"Peters took your mother and me for a chunk of money," Rooster said.

"Really?" I said. "How much?"

"Fifty bucks," my mother said after a sip of wine.

Rooster snorted.

"I think you dropped a few zeros, Maxine," Rooster said.

"Five thousand?" I said.

"I don't want to talk about it."

"Fifty?" I said. "Was it that much?"

"From both of us," Rooster said.

"How did he manage that?" Lacey said.

"With cunning and finesse," Rooster said, then looked at my mother. "I wonder what the heck he's up to now?"

"When we were together, he was trying to reintroduce wolves to the area," Lacey said. "At least his version of the wolf."

Rooster sat back in his chair and stared at my mother.

"Do you buy that story?" he said.

"Not a word of it," my mother said.

"How did you guys cross paths with him?" I said.

"His parents had a summer place up here," my mother said. "Maybe they still do."

"Where?"

"Over on Wellesley, I think," Rooster said.

"We met him at a party," my mother said. "And he told us he was developing a new technology that would remove dangerous particulates from water systems. He sold us on the idea we could be part of a startup with the potential to revolutionize environmental protection efforts. And make a lot of money in the process."

"I take it his project never got off the ground," I said.

"I wouldn't say that," Rooster said. "Since his project turned out to be securing contributions for the Jeremy Peters' retirement fund."

"I can't believe you two got taken in by a con artist," I said.

"He was very convincing," my mother said.

"Did you sue him?" Lacey said.

"We didn't have any basis for a lawsuit," Rooster said. "The contract made it clear it was a startup company with all the associated risks. By the time we figured out what was going on, he'd hit the road." He glanced at Lacey. "He said he was some sort of environmental scientist."

"I'm sure he did," Lacey said with a shrug. "But he got his doctorate in genetics."

"And now he's cross-breeding dogs and wolves?" Josie said.

"He's been doing it for a while," Lacey said.

"Since we found the Utonagan in the area, is it possible Peters is around somewhere?" I said.

"I'd be surprised if he weren't," Lacey said. "Akna was going to be one of the centerpieces of his wolf research."

"Akna?" my mother said.

"That's the dog's name," Lacey said. "I imagine he's been breeding her."

"But how the heck did the dog end up in Sebastian Pines?" I said. "It's so remote."

"If the dog has enough wolf in her, it makes sense," Josie said. "Wolves can have territories that cover hundreds of miles."

28

"They do," Lacey said. "A lot depends on the availability of food."

"What's available around there for them to eat?" my mother said.

"Deer, primarily," Rooster said. "But there are lots of small animals as well. Rabbits, muskrat, stuff like that."

"There's no way that Utonagan preys on other animals, right?" I said, glancing back and forth at Josie and Lacey.

"It's possible," Lacey said. "She's pretty domesticated, but you can't fight genetics. And you saw the way she was looking at some of the smaller dogs at the Inn."

"I did," I said, frowning. "But I still can't figure out how she ended up in Sebastian Pines. It's hundreds of acres of nothing but trees and pasture."

"That's not a lot of ground to cover," Josie said. "If you're a wolf."

"But she's not a wolf," I said. "And the dog is obviously used to being fed by people."

"Maybe the dog got hungry and needed to take things into her own hands," Rooster said.

"Even so, where did she start her trip from?" I said, my neurons firing on all cylinders. "There's nothing out there."

"No, there's not," Rooster said, then cocked his head and frowned. "Except for…" He glanced at my mother who also frowned as she processed his comment.

"Except for what?" I said.

"Is it possible?" my mother said.

"It is relatively close," Rooster said.

"But it's been shut down for what, thirty years?" my mother said, swirling the wine in her glass.

"At least," Rooster said.

"I'm gonna need a little more," I said, growing impatient.

"Cabot Lodge," Rooster said.

"Chocolate jelly beans."

"What?" my mother said.

"Oh, I'm sorry. I thought we were playing the game of inserting random words into conversations," I said. "What the heck is Cabot Lodge?"

"It's an old hunting reserve from back in the seventies," Rooster said.

"Hunting reserve?" Josie said.

"Yeah," Rooster said, nodding. "Some guy created it for people who wanted to hunt in comfort."

"They'd bring in wealthy people to hunt during the day then be pampered at night with food and drink," my mother said. "Wow, talk about a distant memory. I haven't thought about that place in years."

"What happened to it?" I said.

"I imagine they ran out of rich people who wanted to hunt there," Rooster said. "It went out of business, and the guy who owned the place disappeared."

"Who was he?" I said.

"No idea," Rooster said. "If I remember the stories, the owner was a bit of an eccentric. Almost a hermit."

"Wasn't there some sort of accident?" my mother said. "One of the hunters shot somebody or something like that."

"I don't remember," Rooster said. "I was just a kid back then."

"And I wasn't?" my mother said in mock indignation.

Rooster laughed and patted my mother's hand.

"Sorry. You weren't even born yet."

"Well played," my mother said, then tossed back the rest of her wine.

"Smooth," I said, laughing. "What happened to the place after the guy shut it down?"

"I have no idea," Rooster said. "It just sort of came and went. The business didn't last long."

"Could you find it?" I said.

"Here we go," Josie said, shaking her head.

"Shut it."

"I'm sure we could," Rooster said. "All we'd need would be an old map of the area that included the access roads from back then. I imagine they've all been reclaimed by Mother Nature by this point."

"But it's reasonably close to Sebastian Pines?" I said.

"Yeah, I think it is," Rooster said. "It's certainly close enough for the dog to make her way over there from the lodge."

"That settles it then," I said, grabbing my fork.

"Settles what, darling?"

"What I'm going to be doing tomorrow while I wait for the rest of you to find the dog."

Chapter 4

I pulled off the two-lane highway onto a snow-packed access road on the edge of Sebastian Pines. I continued for about a hundred yards then came to a stop and put the SUV in park. But I left the engine running and turned the heater down.

"Your cross-country adventure awaits," I said, climbing out of the car.

"I can't wait," Josie said as she got out. "Tell me again why we can't use a snowmobile?"

"Because you'll freak the dog out," I said.

"Rooster's going to be on a snowmobile," Josie said, protesting.

"Only to scout things out," I said, draping an arm over my mother's shoulder as she leaned in close for warmth. I spotted Rooster's truck making its way toward us, and he came to a stop right behind my SUV and got out. "I thought I lost you."

"Not a chance," he said, pulling a jacket on and zipping it up.

"Look at you," I said. "You're actually appropriately dressed for the weather."

"Well, since I'm spending the day with you, I thought I better be prepared for the worst," he said, pulling a woolen toque over his head and ears.

"Funny. You need any help getting your snowmobile off the trailer?"

"Not from you," he said. "Chef Claire, you mind giving me a hand?"

"You got it."

I watched them expertly maneuver the snowmobile onto the thick snow. Josie removed both pairs of skis from the roof rack and stuck them upright in the snow.

"Okay, how do you want to do this?" Rooster said, staring out at the snow-covered field surrounded on three sides by enormous pine trees.

"Did you bring the walkie-talkies?" I said. "The cell signal might be a bit spotty out here."

"I did," Rooster said, rummaging through a duffel bag and handing one to Josie and another to my mother. "I already set them to the same frequency. All you need to do is turn them on."

"I feel like I'm in a cop show," Chef Claire said.

"A cop show set in the Arctic Circle," Josie said, bouncing up and down on her toes. "Okay, let's get this circus on the road."

"Good idea," I said, grinning. "Then I'm going to get back in the car and have some hot chocolate. But don't worry, you'll warm up as soon as you start trekking toward the pines."

"Enjoy it while you can," Josie said, giving me the evil eye. "You won't be pregnant forever."

"I assume those are your tracks from yesterday," Rooster said, nodding at two sets of ski tracks and a pair of footprints and four smaller tracks next to them.

"They are," Chef Claire said. "We had to walk back after we found the dog."

"What did you use for a leash?"

"A strap from my skis and our belts buckled together," Josie said.

"Well done, Ms. MacGyver," I said.

"I'm really not in the mood, Suzy," Josie said. "And to think I could be in Grand Cayman sipping an umbrella drink."

"Where's the fun in that? Okay, Rooster. What do you think?"

"Well, since the assumption is the dog is going to head back to where you found her, I think Josie and Chef Claire should follow their tracks from yesterday. I'll work the outside edges of the pines and see if I can spot her with the binoculars. If I do, I'll get on the radio. We'll come up with a plan from there."

"Okay, let's do this," Josie said, kneeling down to slip her skis on.

"What are you guys going to be doing?" Rooster said.

"I thought we'd follow this access road as far as it goes and see where it leads," I said, glancing at my mother. "You got the map, right?"

"I do," she said.

"I'm not sure how we're going to find another access road in two feet of snow, but maybe we'll get lucky."

"Are you sure you're okay being out here?" Rooster said.

"We'll be fine, Rooster," my mother said.

"Absolutely," I said. "We've got a full tank of gas, four-wheel drive, and enough food for a week."

"Not to mention you're one radio call away," my mother said. "Okay, I'm officially cold. Let's go, darling." She waved to the others. "Have fun out there."

Rooster held my arm as I slowly made my way back into the driver seat and gently closed the door behind me. I turned the heat up then glanced over at my mother who was already studying the map.

"It looks like you're really into this adventure, Mom."

"Actually, I am," she said. "And if we do happen to run into Peters, I'd hate to miss it."

"Fifty grand. It's still bugging you, huh?"

"It's not the money, darling. It's the idea I let myself get conned by that sleazeball that bugs me."

"I can see that. Are you ready?"

"Hang on a sec," she said, pouring hot chocolate into two travel mugs. She handed me one then took a sip of hers. "Okay, let's do this."

I put the SUV in gear, and we slowly made our way across the snowy field. I looked out the window and spotted Josie and Chef Claire working their way toward the pines. Rooster's snowmobile was already a distant speck.

"You think we're still actually on the access road?" I said.

"Hard to tell," my mother said. "Just take your time in case we aren't."

"I feel bad about leaving Lacey alone at the Inn on her first day."

"I'm sure she'll be fine, darling. And Sammy and Jill are there to handle any questions she might have."

"Yeah, you're right. I like her."

"Me too," my mother said, then grabbed her travel mug with both hands when the SUV bounced over the uneven terrain. "Easy, Leadfoot."

"Sorry. It sounds like her relationship with Peters ended badly."

"How could it not? The man is despicable."

"Then how could she have gotten involved with him in the first place?"

"Like I said last night, he's very convincing."

"Got it."

Our walkie-talkie squawked then we heard Rooster's voice.

"How's it going?"

"Nothing yet," I said.

"We're almost to the pines," Chef Claire said. "It's so beautiful out here. And what a great workout."

I could hear the sound of her skis cutting through the snow.

"Isn't it, Josie?" Chef Claire said.

I heard Josie's muffled response through the radio.

"What did she say?"

"Oh, I'm not comfortable using that sort of language," Chef Claire said, laughing.

"I'm at the far edge of the pines and about to start working my way into the trees," Rooster said.

"We're still following the access road. At least, I think we are," I said.

"Okay. I'll check in again soon," Rooster said.

My mother picked up a pair of binoculars then glanced over.

"Let's stop for a sec while I take a look."

"I think I'll join you," I said, coming to a stop and putting the SUV in park. I rummaged through the duffel bag until I found another pair of binoculars. I scanned the horizon through the windshield but came up empty. "Well, if there's another access road around here, I sure don't see it."

"Let's take a look at the map," she said, spreading it across her lap. "We must be around here, right?"

"I think so," I said, leaning over to take a closer look. Then I pointed at a spot on the map. "Right there."

"I'm not following," she said, frowning.

"Do you see where the pines on the map form a little curlicue on the right edge of the forest?"

"I do," she said, staring down at the map.

"Now, look at those trees about a hundred yards up on our right," I said, reaching for my binoculars.

"Good eye, darling," she said, staring through the binoculars. "I think you're right. It's the section of pines where those snowdrifts have accumulated."

"Yeah," I said, sweeping the binoculars back and forth.

"Those are some big drifts," she said. "Which makes sense given all the snow we've had this winter."

"Take a closer look, Mom."

"What?"

"What's odd about those drifts?"

My mother continued to stare through the binoculars then lowered them and looked over at me.

"The crests of the drifts are going in the wrong direction."

"Exactly. With the prevailing winds out here, the drifts should be curved the other way," I said, my neurons surging. "Those aren't natural."

"They were made by a snowplow on the other side of the trees. How did you do that?"

"Lucky guess," I said, shrugging. "There's just one problem."

"What's that?"

"How the heck do we get to the other side?"

Chapter 5

I grabbed the walkie-talkie and pressed the talk button.

"Hello? Anybody there?"

"Winter Wonderland Pizza. Will this be for pick-up or delivery?" Josie said.

"Funny," I said, accepting the sandwich my mother was holding out. "Where are you guys?"

"Well, I can't speak for Chef Claire, but I'm on the border of a meltdown."

"What's the problem?"

"I'm standing in the middle of a forest in February freezing my butt off. What the hell do you think the problem is?"

"A little snarky today, huh?" I said, grinning at my mother.

"What's going on?" Josie said.

"Actually, I was calling Rooster."

"Hey," Rooster said above the noise of the idling snowmobile. "How's it going?"

"I think we might have found another access road," I said, then took a big bite of my sandwich. "But we can't get at it."

"Hang on," Rooster said. "You're breaking up."

"Sorry," I said, swallowing. "It looks like there's a road on the other side of us that's been plowed."

"Where are you?"

"We're at the end of the tree line right where it starts to curve back toward the highway," I said.

"Okay," Rooster said. "I'll be there in five. Josie, have you guys seen anything yet?"

"Just a bunch of animal tracks," Josie said.

"What kind?" Rooster said.

"All creatures great and small," she said. "There's some sort of underground spring near here. I imagine all the critters are drinking from it."

"Any sign of the dog?" I said.

"No. Just some tracks that look like they could be hers," Josie said. "I think it's a dead end."

"How about I pick you guys up on the way?" Rooster said.

"Oh, not the briar patch."

"Just stay put," he said. "I'll follow your tracks."

"You can't miss us," Josie said.

"Okay," Rooster said. "Suzy, we'll be there in about ten minutes."

"Not a problem," I said, then set the walkie-talkie down and attacked my sandwich.

"This is delicious," my mother said. "The mayo has dill and mint, right?"

"Yeah. And I think she added a pinch of saffron," I said. "Odd combination, but it works."

"It always does."

We chatted while we finished our sandwiches. A few minutes later, I flinched.

"What's the matter, darling?"

"The baby's kicking."

"Let me feel," she said, gently placing a hand on my stomach. "Wow. She's really going at it."

"I think she liked the sandwich," I said, then laughed.

The purr of a snowmobile engine caught our attention, and we watched Rooster slowly make his way down the edge of the tree line. Chef Claire was sitting behind him with her arms wrapped around his waist. Josie sat behind her holding both pairs of skis.

"He's an amazing man," I said, watching how carefully he was driving the large machine.

"He certainly is."

"How come the two of you never hooked up, Mom?"

"And ruin a beautiful friendship?"

I laughed and patted her knee.

"How long did it take you guys to figure out you were better off as friends?"

"Not long," she said with a shrug. "It was an easy decision for both of us."

"How long have you two known each other?"

"Geez, since we were kids. It must be coming up on fifty years."

"Are you ever going to tell me the story about how the two of you made some of your money?"

"There's really not a lot to tell, darling," she said, deflecting my question.

"Okay, whatever you say, Mom," I said, opening the door when the snowmobile came to a stop next to the SUV. I climbed out and zipped my coat up. "Welcome back."

"It was great," Chef Claire said, her face flushed bright pink from the cold and wind.

"Truly magical," Josie said with a shake of her head as she climbed into the SUV.

"So, what did you find?" Rooster said, turning the snowmobile off and getting to his feet.

"It's right over there," I said, pointing. "That looks like something a snowplow would leave behind, doesn't it?"

"It certainly does," he said, glancing around. "But I don't see a road. Maybe we're looking at a spot where the road bends."

"That's what I was thinking," I said. "But where the heck does the access road start? It must connect to the highway at some point."

"There's only one way to find out," Rooster said, walking back to the snowmobile.

"You're going up and over the snowbank?"

"That's the plan," he said, starting the engine. "Why don't you get back in the car and stay warm? I'll be back soon."

I watched as he slowly headed for the large bank of snow, worked the machine up the side, then disappeared from sight. I listened to the sound of the engine that was barely above an idle for several seconds then came to life with a throaty roar. Assuming he'd found something worth exploring on the other side, I worked my way into the driver seat. Josie and Chef Claire were sitting in the back eating.

"Amazing sandwich, Chef Claire," I said.

"Thanks," she said through a mouthful. "It's so beautiful out here."

Josie glanced over at her but said nothing. She polished off her sandwich. "What's for dessert?"

"Brownies," Chef Claire said.

"Maybe there is a chance to save the day," Josie said, groaning as she reached for the backpack. "My legs are on fire."

"It's good for you," Chef Claire said. "It builds character."

"You're so weird," Josie said, offering brownies to everyone.

We sat quietly as we ate. A few minutes later, Rooster's voice came through the walkie-talkie.

"I found it," he said.

"The entrance to another access road?" I said.

"Yeah," Rooster said. "It's pretty well hidden."

"Is it off Johnson Springs road?"

"No, it's actually off Billingsley."

"I'm not familiar with it," I said, frowning and glancing over at my mother.

"I don't see any road signs," she said, studying the map.

"All you need to do is turn around and get back to the road we came in on," Rooster said. "Make a left, and you'll run into Johnson Springs."

"Yeah, I get that," I said.

"Then you're going to see a one-lane road about a mile up. That's Billingsley. Make a left. About a half-mile up, you're going to start seeing a fence line. Turn into the first gap in the fence you see. I'll be waiting there."

"That's three lefts in a row," I said. "So, I'll be driving in a circle?"

"Pretty much," Rooster said.

"Has the road been plowed?"

"It's definitely been plowed most of the winter," he said. "But the last snowfall wasn't cleared."

"When was that?" I said. "A couple of days ago?"

"Yeah, we got four inches the other night," Rooster said. "I'll see you when you get here. Save me a sandwich."

I carefully turned the SUV around and followed Rooster's directions. About fifteen minutes later, I finally located the entrance and inched the vehicle through a small opening. A hundred feet away, I spotted Rooster stretched out on the seat of the snow machine. He got to his feet when he spotted us. I lowered my window.

"You want to get in?" I said. "You must be freezing."

"No, I'm fine," he said. "But I will take one of those sandwiches."

I handed him one, and he took a big bite. Then he pointed off into the distance.

"That's the spot where you just came from. It's one hell of a snowbank."

"It certainly is," I said, following his eyes. "Somebody has been using the road all winter."

"That's my guess," he said, taking another bite and giving Chef Claire a thumbs up. "The road bends to the right. As soon as I finish my sandwich, I'll lead the way."

"Take your time," I said.

"Yeah, like that's gonna happen," he said, then laughed and took another big bite. "Who the heck would choose to spend the winter out here?"

"Given how remote it is, I imagine it's somebody who doesn't want anybody to know they're here."

"Yeah. Or somebody who's a hermit," Rooster said, glancing around the immediate area. "Well, what do you know?"

"What is it?"

"Dog tracks," Rooster said, pointing.

Chapter 6

I followed the snowmobile at a safe distance, glancing around my surroundings as we headed deeper into the forest. The road was covered with fresh snow but hardpacked underneath. As such, the four-wheel drive SUV didn't have any problems navigating the small, one-lane road. The dog tracks were easy to follow as we continued our journey.

"It's amazing," Chef Claire said, glancing out through the windows. "It's like a postcard."

"If we see Santa and his elves, I'm gonna freak out," Josie said, shaking her head. "I know we live in a rural area, but this is nuts. It's like civilization skipped this place."

"If you were setting up a hunting reserve, I imagine privacy is pretty high on the list," Chef Claire said.

"I used to drive the back roads all the time after I got my license," I said. "I can't believe I missed this one."

"You were probably more focused on who was in the car with you," my mother said. "That would have been Billy, right?"

"No, I'd broken up with him by that point," I said, glancing over at her. "I was dating Jeff the first year I had my license. Geez, there's a blast from the past. I wonder whatever happened to him."

"You little heartbreaker," Josie said with a laugh.

"No, it was nothing like that," I said, glancing at her through the rear-view mirror. "We decided we were better off as friends."

"How did you figure that out?" my mother said.

"The hard way."

I slowed down when I saw Rooster pull off to the side of the narrow road and come to a stop. I put the SUV in park, and we all climbed out. I immediately spotted a large stone structure about a hundred yards in front of us.

"Cabot Lodge, I presume?" I said.

"That would be my guess," Rooster said. "It looks like it's in pretty good shape."

"Those granite walls aren't going anywhere," I said.

"New roof," my mother said, pointing at what was obviously a recent upgrade.

"Okay," I said. "Color me intrigued." I glanced around at them. "Should we walk in or drive?"

"Really?" Josie said, climbing into the backseat.

We all followed suit, and I made the short drive. I parked next to Rooster's snowmobile. I got out and studied the outside of the structure.

"No smoke coming from the chimney," I said. "Is it possible the place has a power supply?"

"Sure," Rooster said. "It would have been expensive to put in when they built the place, but it wouldn't have been a problem."

"I don't hear a generator," I said. Then I shrugged. "Let's go check it out. Lead the way, Rooster."

My mother and Josie each grabbed one of my arms and led me up the front steps onto a large porch. Various pieces of outdoor furniture were scattered around covered with tarps which were covered with snow.

"It's nice," I said, taking another look around.

"Peaceful," Chef Claire said.

"So was the Cabin in the Woods," Josie said. "This place gives me the creeps."

"You're such a baby," I said, gently punching her on the shoulder. "Is the front door locked?"

"It is not," my mother said, slowly opening the door and peering inside.

We all entered and stood in the foyer taking the place in. Stone and wood dominated and the living room had a vaulted ceiling. The place had a distinct musty smell, but I couldn't miss the faint trace of smoke. A large fireplace had a covering of ashes, and a stack of firewood sat nearby. I flipped a light switch, and we were immediately bathed in light.

"You want to take the tour or should we split up?" I said, glancing around.

"I'll check out the upstairs," Rooster said, pointing at a large wooden staircase. "You guys take a look around down here."

"I'll go with you," Chef Claire said.

We watched them head upstairs then walked across the enormous living room. A large country kitchen appeared. I opened the fridge and found it fully stocked. A second fridge was filled with various plastic bags of raw meat.

"That's a lot of meat," my mother said. "Maybe he's planning a party."

"Or he's feeding a lot of dogs," I said, closing the door.

"Or wolves," Josie said.

Rooster and Chef Claire came down the staircase and entered the kitchen.

"Looks like seven bedrooms," Rooster said. "But only one of them is being used at the moment."

"The place is incredible," Chef Claire said. "A bit rundown, but very livable."

"Let's check out the backyard," I said, heading down a hallway.

I led the way down a long hallway adorned with faded, framed photos from a time long gone. The door that opened onto the back porch was unlocked, and I stepped outside, totally unprepared for what I saw. Off to our left was a row of wire cages. I studied the occupants then looked at Josie who was shaking her head.

"I think we got here just in time," she said, exhaling loudly.

I nodded my agreement then spotted something at the bottom of the stairs.

"Geez," I whispered. "Rooster, would you mind checking that out?"

"Yeah, I got it," he said, slowly making his way down the steps.

"Is that who I think it is?" my mother called out to Rooster.

He was kneeling over the body and taking a close look without touching it. He stood and nodded as he looked up at us.

"Yeah, it's Peters," Rooster said. "It looks like he's been here a couple of days at least."

"What do you see?" I said.

"It's a bit hard to tell with all the snow. But he's got a pretty big wound to the back of his head."

"Shot?" I said.

"No, I don't think so. It looks like he was hit with something," Rooster said. "Or he fell down the stairs and managed to do it to himself."

"How likely is that?" I said, studying the long flight of stairs.

"On a scale between one and ten, probably less than zero."

"We need to get hold of the Chief," I said, then checked my phone. "I can't get a signal."

"Me either," Josie said.

"Mom, Josie and I need to check out those cages. Could you go inside and see if Peters had a computer?"

"You want me to email the Chief?" she said.

"Yeah, tell him what we found and have him bring Detective Williams from the state police with him. The Chief won't have any jurisdiction out here."

"I can do that," my mother said, heading for the back door.

"Oh, Mom. Ask them to swing by the Inn and bring Lacey with them. She might have some sort of idea about what we're dealing with."

"Okay," she said, glancing down at the row of cages. "You think they're wolves?"

"My guess is they have some percentage of wolf in them," I said.

"Except for those two," Josie said, pointing. "I'm betting those guys are one hundred percent wolf."

"Just keep your distance," my mother said as she headed inside the lodge.

I grabbed the railing and slowly worked my way down the stairs. Rooster met me halfway and held my other arm until I reached the bottom step. Josie and Chef Claire followed me, and we approached the cages. There were a dozen, all identical. Each of the chain-link cages contained a wooden structure with an opening.

"At least they have a place to get out of the cold," Josie said, surveying the scene.

"We need to feed them," I said. "It's probably been a day or two since they've eaten."

"I'll go grab some of the bags of meat we saw in the fridge," Josie said.

"No, I'll get it," Chef Claire said. "You guys stay here and see what you can figure out."

She headed up the stairs as Josie and I began a slow stroll toward the row of cages. Half of them were occupied by a single animal. The others had two or more, except for the last cage that appeared empty. Most of the occupants hung back as if not knowing what to expect from their uninvited guests. The animal in the first cage bared its teeth and maintained a low, steady growl as we approached.

"Easy, big guy," Josie said softly as she came to a stop outside the cage. "That is a wolf. Probably the alpha."

"Well, he's certainly not a lap dog," I said, keeping a close eye on him. "They all seem to be different ages."

"Yeah, I noticed," she said, moving down a cage where three animals were warily staring back. "How many generations do you think we're looking at?"

"It has to be at least three."

"Sounds about right," Josie said, then shook her head and pointed. "No, make that four."

We stared into the last cage. Inside the wooden structure was an adult who was hunkered down and obviously protecting a litter of pups.

"Wolf puppies are born deaf and blind, right?"

"They are," Josie said, craning her neck to get a better look inside the doghouse. "They open their eyes after a couple of weeks. After three to four weeks, they take their first walk out of the den."

"You got any idea how old they are?" I said.

"No, I can't get a good look. But they're definitely young."

"Isn't it a bit early in the year for her to be having pups?"

"A little," Josie said. "They usually give birth in the spring. But since this isn't a natural environment for them, it's not that unusual. Especially if this guy Peters was orchestrating things."

"The poor animals," I said, then stared off into the distance.

"What's the matter?"

"I'm just wondering what percentage of wolf they are," I said.

"You mean, has Peters been trying to increase or decrease the amount of wolf in each generation?"

"Yeah, that would be good to know before we start interacting with them."

"You, my friend, won't be interacting with any of them," Josie said. "At least until we're positive we know what they are."

"We could have some genetic testing done on them," I said.

"My guess is that Peters has already done that. He's probably got it all written down somewhere."

"That makes sense," I said, nodding as I spotted my mother and Chef Claire heading down the stairs.

Rooster joined them as they made the short walk to the cages.

"The good news is that he had a computer," my mother said. "Bad news is it's password protected."

"I'll head out until I get coverage," Rooster said, zipping his coat up. "Then I'll wait for them by the access road."

"You sure?" I said. "It's cold and you'll be waiting for quite a while."

"I'll be fine," Rooster said. "But I will take one of those sandwiches with me."

He headed off with a wave, and we heard the sound of the snowmobile as he drove off. Chef Claire, holding several bags of meat, glanced up and down the row of cages.

"How do we do this?" she said, handing a bag to each of us.

"There's a slot in each cage," Josie said. "Just toss a bunch in. They're obviously starving. But do not, and I can't stress this enough, put your hands inside."

"What on earth was he doing?" my mother said, surveying the row of cages.

"It looks like he's been breeding hybrids," I said, reaching into the bag and removing a large chunk of raw meat. I grinned at Josie. "Now, this is for these guys. Don't get any ideas."

"Funny," Josie said, pushing a large chunk through one of the openings. "It smells okay."

"Yeah, it's pretty fresh," Chef Claire said.

We watched the wolf-dogs devour their dinner. Except for the mother of the pups. She stayed inside the doghouse and glanced back and forth between us and the large chunk of meat Josie had thrown in.

"She's not going to eat while we're standing here," Josie said. "Let's head inside and give her some privacy."

"You'll get no argument from me," my mother said as she headed for the stairs.

Back inside, Josie and Chef Claire went to work building a fire. I watched from the comfort of a couch as my mom went exploring. A few minutes later, Josie and Chef Claire put the finishing touches on the fire and sat down next to me.

"Promise me something," Josie said, patting my belly.

"What's that?"

"Don't go into labor out here."

"I'll do my best."

Chapter 7

My mother returned about fifteen minutes later shaking her head.

"The guy has the place stocked to the rafters with provisions," she said. "There's enough food here to last a couple of years. If it weren't for the wolfdogs, I'd swear the guy was one of those survivalists."

"What on earth was he doing living way out here?" Chef Claire said.

"An eccentric nutjob performing science experiments on animals wanting to stay below the radar?" Josie said. "I can make it work."

"Yeah," I said, glancing around the lodge. "Do you think he owned this place?"

"I have no idea," my mother said. "I thought it would be in ruins by this point."

"Do you think somebody killed him?" Chef Claire said.

"I don't think his head got bashed in just from falling down the stairs," I said.

"But who'd want to kill him?" Chef Claire said.

"My money's on Wolfman," Josie deadpanned. "Maybe Peters was cutting into his territory."

"Really? That's the best you got?" I said with a grin.

"I feel like a glass of wine," Chef Claire said.

"Great idea," my mother said. "I'm sure he won't mind."

Chef Claire headed to the kitchen and returned with a bottle and three glasses. She handed me a glass of sparkling water then poured the wine. We sat quietly enjoying our drinks and the fire until we heard Rooster's snowmobile approaching the lodge. It was soon followed by the sound of a vehicle. We heard muffled conversations then the sound of footsteps on the front porch. Chef Claire opened the door and greeted all four.

"Geez," Chief Abrams grunted as he headed for the fireplace and looked around. "What a place."

"Man, when you said remote hunting lodge, you weren't kidding," Freddie said. "I can't believe you even found it."

"Hey, Lacey," I said. "How did it go today?"

"It was great," she said. "I spent the day playing with several dozen dogs. How bad could it be?"

"Sorry to ruin it," I said. "Hi, Detective Williams."

"Hey, Suzy," he said, nodding and waving to everyone. "Long time, no see."

"It's been a few months," I said. "How have you been?"

"Apart from dealing with the winter doldrums, not bad," Detective Williams said. "Where's the body?"

"Back deck. At the bottom of the stairs," Rooster said, motioning for them to follow him.

"Is it really Jeremy?" Lacey said.

"I'm afraid so," I said.

She teared up and wiped at her eyes with a sleeve.

"Okay, let's do this," Detective Williams said, following Rooster down the hall.

I slowly worked myself off the couch onto my feet.

"Where do you think you're going?" my mother said.

"Relax, Mom. I'm just going to listen in," I said, glancing back over my shoulder.

"Just promise to behave yourself, darling." She glanced at Josie and Chef Claire. "Should we tag along or sit here in front of the fire enjoying our wine?"

"I don't need to see the body again," Josie said, frowning at my mother.

"Yeah, it's kind of a false choice, Mrs. C.," Chef Claire said, taking a sip of wine.

"Silly me," my mother said, propping her feet up on the footstool directly in front of her.

I stepped onto the back porch and zipped my coat up. I bounced on my toes and hugged myself for warmth as I watched the two cops and Freddie study the body of Dr. Jeremy Peters at the bottom of the stairs. Lacey remained on the porch with me, the blank look on her face a mixture of confusion and despair.

"Did you know about this place?"

"No," Lacey whispered. "We called it quits before he got bounced out of Copeland. He said he was heading west."

"It looks like he changed his mind."

"If Jeremy was anything, he was unpredictable," she said, then finally spotted the cages. "How many are here?"

"Looks like around twenty," I said. "Not counting the litter of pups in the last cage."

"What a mess," she said, shaking her head. "How many generations do you think there are?"

"Our best guess is three, maybe four."

"And all different percentages of wolf."

"Probably," I said, studying the male in the first cage that was keeping a close eye on all of us. I spotted Freddie brushing away the snow near the body. A large, jagged rock came into view. "Interesting."

"What?" Lacey said, her eyes following mine.

"The rock at the bottom of the stairs," I said, then called out. "Freddie, does that rock have blood on it?"

"A little," he said without looking up from what he was doing.

"You think he fell and hit his head?" Lacey said.

"No, I don't. But somebody might have wanted us to think that," Freddie said.

"He was murdered?" Lacey whispered.

"That's my first guess," I said, again bouncing on my toes. "Any idea who might want to kill him?"

"Ex-girlfriend. His wife. Business partners. Irate husbands. People he swindled money out of," Lacey said. "Should I continue?"

"Got it," I said.

"The thought also crossed my mind from time to time," she said, then caught the look I was giving her. "Metaphorically speaking, of course."

Chief Abrams led the way up the stairs. Detective Williams and Freddie followed. The state policeman studied the top step then looked down at the body. He repeated it several times with a frown on his face.

"I don't know, Chief," he said. "I suppose it's possible. What do you think, Freddie?"

"That he did a header down the stairs and landed on that rock?" the medical examiner said. "If he slipped and bounced down the stairs, I'd say no. He wouldn't have generated enough speed on his way down to create a head wound that big. But if he somehow managed to miss the top step and fall through the air the whole way, maybe."

"How long has he been dead?" I said.

"My best guess is a couple of days," Freddie said. "But since he's been outside in this cold, it's hard to tell at the moment."

Josie stepped out onto the porch and shivered.

"How's it going?"

"We were just discussing the possibility Peters fell down the stairs and hit his head," Chief Abrams said.

"And?" Josie said.

The two cops looked at each other, then focused on Freddie who gave it some thought then shrugged.

"It's remote. At best," he said. "A shovel or a piece of firewood is more likely."

"Yeah," Detective Williams said, nodding. He stared off into the distance then appeared to notice the cages for the first time. "The guy was a dog lover, huh?"

"That's debatable," Josie said. "He was breeding dogs with wolves."

"What?" the detective said with a deep frown.

"Yeah, hybrids," I said.

"To what end?" Detective Williams said.

"He was trying to come up with a hybrid that could live in the wild but still be socialized enough to live around people," Lacey said.

"Excuse me if this sounds intrusive, but how the heck do you know that?"

"I used to work for him," Lacey said softly. "And we dated for a while."

"How long ago was this?" the detective said.

"I called it off a couple years ago," she said.

"And you just moved to the area? Right around the time he died?"

"Easy, Detective Williams," I said.

"I'm just asking," he said, staring at me.

"It's okay, Suzy," Lacey said. "It's a logical question to ask. Yes, Detective. I just moved to the area to work for Suzy and Josie. But I didn't have a clue Jeremy was living around here."

"Okay," Detective Williams said. "But I'm sure we're going to have some questions for you."

"I'd be surprised if you didn't," she said.

"Can we continue this conversation inside?" Chief Abrams said.

"What a good idea," Josie said, wheeling around and heading for the door.

We followed and I stood in front of the fire to warm myself up. Then I flinched and pressed a hand on my stomach.

"What's the matter, darling?" my mother said, immediately on point.

"The baby is kicking," I said. "Relax, Mom."

"We should get going," she said. "You don't need us, right, Chief?"

"No, you guys are good to go whenever you're ready," Chief Abrams said.

"Aren't you forgetting something?" Detective Williams said.

"The hybrids," I said, nodding.

"I assume you'll be taking them to your place," the detective said.

Josie and I shook our heads in unison.

"Not a chance," Josie said.

"But you're the dog people," Detective Williams said. "Why not?"

"Because we don't know what we're dealing with," I said. "We can't take the risk."

"Risk? What are you talking about?"

"Peters has been breeding wolves with dogs," Josie said. "And until we know the genetics of each hybrid, there's no way we can keep them at the Inn."

"I'm not following you," Detective Williams said.

"Just because an animal is socialized, it doesn't mean its instincts are negated. Wolves are predators. And we have a lot of dogs, particularly smaller ones, who could be in danger," I said. "Not a chance we're taking them back to our place."

"Is there anybody around the area who could take them?" the detective said.

"I seriously doubt it," Josie said. "And I wouldn't be comfortable recommending that option."

"Okay," Detective Williams said. "Hey, you guys also have a rescue center. You've got a ton of acreage. Couldn't you put them there?"

"Absolutely not," I said. "As soon as spring gets here, we're going to have families with young kids visiting."

"Just leave them in a cage," the detective said with a shrug.

"They're already in a cage," Josie said. "They need to be put somewhere where they can run."

"And that's the problem," I said.

"You got that right," Josie said.

"I think I'm going to need a bit more," Chief Abrams said.

"Those hybrids out there are caught between a rock and a hard place. They'd have a tough time surviving in the wild. Especially since they're used to being hand fed. And there's no way we can let people adopt them."

"Then we'll just put them down," Detective Williams said, shrugging it off.

"Over my dead body," Josie snapped.

"What she said," I said, glaring at the cop.

"Oh, you were doing so well up to that point, Detective," my mother said, laughing.

"Yeah, I knew it as soon as it came out of my mouth," the detective said, grinning at her. "Okay, then. What do you suggest we do with them?"

"We'll just leave them here," Lacey said.

"Great idea," Josie said. "We can take turns coming out here to feed them until we get a better idea of what we're dealing with."

"No, there's no need for that," Lacey said. "I'll just stay here. I need a place to live. As long as we don't get any more storms, I'll be able to get in and out."

"Peters' truck is in the garage," Rooster said. "And it has a snowplow on the front."

"He was plowing his own road," I said. "Apparently, he thought of everything."

"It would be okay for me to stay here, wouldn't it?" Lacey said, glancing back and forth at both cops. "You know, from a legal standpoint."

"I don't see why not," the Chief said. "At least until we find out if the guy had a will."

"Or if he even owned the place," I said.

"I don't know," Detective Williams said. "If Peters was murdered, there's always a chance whoever did it might come back."

"I'll stay here with her," Rooster said.

"You will?" Chief Abrams said.

"Sure. It'll give me something to do other than watch TV," Rooster said, then glanced at Lacey. "If it's okay with you."

"I don't have a problem with it," she said. "It'll be good to have some company."

"That settles it," Rooster said, then looked at me. "You mind taking care of my guys for a few days?"

"Not at all," I said. "We'll swing by and pick them up on our way home."

"Okay," Detective Williams said. "But if you see anybody hanging around, let us know right away."

"I'll ride back with you," Rooster said. "I'll leave my snowmobile here. We might need it at some point." He looked at Lacey. "What kind of car do you have?"

"A four-wheel drive SUV," she said. "I'll be fine."

"We'll pick up our cars and caravan back. We should get going. I'd like to get settled in before it gets dark."

"Sounds like a plan," Lacey said. "We might need to shop for food."

"No, you're fine," my mother said. "The place is stocked." She focused on the cops. "Gentlemen, we are going to head out. You must have a ton of work left to do."

"I'll need a ride," Freddie said. "I've got to grab some folks then get back out here to remove the body."

"Detective Williams and I will wait until you get back, Rooster," the Chief said. "While you're gone, we'll see if we can make some sense out of this."

"Good luck," I said, shaking my head. "Okay, let's hit the road. All we need to do is figure out how to fit seven people in the SUV."

Josie sidled up next to Rooster and gave him an evil grin.

"Your new roomie can sit on your lap," she whispered.

"Shut it," Rooster said, then laughed.

"Some people will do anything for a date," I said, grinning at him.

"I repeat, shut it."

"A cozy cabin in the woods. A nice bottle of wine. A roaring fire," Josie said.

"Hey, I could do a lot worse," Rooster said.

"So could she," I said, gently punching him on the shoulder.

Chapter 8

By noon the next day, Josie and I were back at Cabot Lodge chatting with Lacey about her first impressions of the hybrids. The Chief and Rooster were inside exploring the house for clues.

"So, he was definitely murdered?" Lacey said as she continued tossing chunks of raw meat through the slots in the cages.

"Yeah, he was," I said. "Freddie called the Chief last night. He found traces of wood embedded in the back of his head."

"Geez, Jeremy. What on earth were you up to?" Lacey said, her eyes wet and wide. "Have they found the murder weapon?"

"No," I said. "The Chief thinks whoever killed him probably just tossed it in the fireplace."

"Burn the evidence," Lacey said, nodding. "That makes sense."

"What's your take on these guys so far?" Josie said.

"From what I can tell, the two males are definitely pure wolf," Lacey said. "Or very close to it. The others all have some percentage of wolf in them."

"How can you be so sure?" I said.

"It's the way they're all skittish when people are around," Lacey said. "Most dogs love being around people or are at least willing to check them out. These guys all hang back when we're out here."

"The males are definitely on guard," Josie said. "What's the word I'm looking for?"

"Wary," I said, returning the stare one of the males was giving me. "Have you seen the Utonagan?"

"No, she's not around anywhere," Lacey said.

"What the heck are we going to do with them?" Josie said, glancing down the row of cages. "There's no way we could ever feel comfortable letting anybody adopt them."

"No, there's not," I said, then headed for the stairs that led to the back porch. "We'll figure something out. Let's get out of this cold."

We walked inside, and I left Josie and Lacey in the kitchen making coffee while I went looking for the Chief. I heard him and Rooster upstairs. I took one look at the long staircase that led to the second floor and decided I could wait for their update. I wandered down a hall and came to a home office. Sitting behind the desk was a tech from the state police I'd met before. I knocked softly. He looked up and waved me in.

"Hey, Suzy. Wow, look at you. You must be getting close, huh?"

"Hi, Jimbo," I said, slowly making my way to the desk. "Yeah, it won't be long now. And I can't wait."

"Sure, I get that," Jimbo Walker said. "My wife loves being pregnant, but near the end, she can't wait for it to be over."

"How many kids do you guys have now?"

"Five," he said, rocking back and forth in the leather chair. "And we're done."

"Is it okay for me to sit down?"

"Sure. I just finished dusting for prints," he said. "Knock yourself out."

I sat down and looked around the office. A large bookshelf filled with academic-looking textbooks dominated one wall. Various framed photographs hung on another. Apart from the computer, the desktop was clear and polished.

"Interesting," I said.

"What's that?" Jimbo said without looking up from the collection of fingerprints he was organizing into a stack.

"Peters was supposedly eccentric," I said. "But this doesn't look like the office of a scatterbrain."

"No, it doesn't," Jimbo said, finally looking up from his work. "But it takes all kinds, right?"

"Yeah, I suppose it does. Were you able to get into his computer?"

"No, it's password protected, and I couldn't find it anywhere," he said. "As soon as Detective Williams gets a search warrant, we'll be taking it."

"Does he even need a warrant?" I said, frowning. "It's a murder investigation."

"He's playing it by the book," Jimbo said. "You know Detective Williams. Better safe than sorry."

"Is that Peters' phone?"

"Yeah. Same deal. Password protected. But it doesn't matter. We'll be able to get at all his stuff. It's just going to take some time," Jimbo said, getting to his feet. "Okay, I'm gonna get out of here. My kid has a hockey game at three, and I need to drop these prints off first."

"Nice seeing you, Jimbo."

"You too, Suzy. Hey, is it true the guy was breeding wolves with dogs?"

"It certainly looks like it."

"Why can't people just leave Mother Nature alone?"

"He was a genetic engineer. I imagine he couldn't help himself," I said with a shrug.

"Well, you and Josie are the experts on our four-legged friends," he said, pausing at the door. "What are you going to do with them?"

"I have no idea," I said. "The animals are between a rock and a hard place."

"I'm sure you'll figure something out."

"Is it okay if I poke around in here?"

"Sure," he said, laughing. "I've got all I need. But Detective Williams said he was coming out later this afternoon. And you might want to be done snooping by the time he gets here. He's pretty protective about his investigations."

"Yes, I know," I said, grinning at him.

"I'm sure you do," Jimbo said. "Have fun. And good luck with the baby."

"Thanks, Jimbo," I said, waving.

After he left the office, I picked up Peters' phone and turned it on. The screen blinked, waiting for the password. I set the phone down on the desk and focused on the computer. It was a laptop connected to two monitors. I turned it on and was soon staring at another screen, also waiting for a password. I rummaged through the desk looking for something the passwords might be written on but came up empty. I was staring off into space drumming my fingers on the desk when Chief Abrams entered.

"Hey, what are you doing?" he said, approaching the desk and sitting down across from me.

"Just trying to figure out where Peters might have written down his passwords."

"Did Jimbo give you permission to be poking around in here?" he said, raising an eyebrow at me.

"Permission is such a strong term, Chief."

"Suzy," he said, his voice rising in warning.

"Relax. He said it was okay. He's got all he needs. But he had to leave everything here until Detective Williams gets a search warrant."

"Yeah, he's a stickler when it comes to stuff like that," Chief Abrams said, placing a leather-bound journal on the desk.

"I see you've been snooping around as well," I said, nodding at the journal.

"I'm a cop. I don't snoop. I investigate."

"Okay, Columbo. Whatever you say. What is that thing?"

"A journal I found in the nightstand next to his bed," the Chief said. "The late-night random musings of a nutjob. There's some weird stuff in it."

I flipped through the journal, pausing to read random selections. I frowned and read a snippet a second time.

"Tame the present to formulate the future. Isolate cruel randomness and destroy it now. A better tomorrow for those who dare to create. Don't ask why. Just ask how."

"Not exactly the lyrics to a country song," the Chief said.

"At least it rhymes," I said with a laugh. I continued flipping through the pages and landed on an elaborate drawing that seemed to fold back on itself. "Did you see this one? It looks like one of those M.C. Escher drawings."

"I always liked his stuff," Chief Abrams said. "Hands drawing hands. Staircases that appear to go up and down at the same time. Let me see it."

I handed the journal to the Chief who studied the page closely. "It's a combination of letters and numbers. I can't quite make it out."

"It says Project Org 2020," I said.

"Okay, yeah, now I see it," he said, handing the journal back. "But what the heck does it mean?"

"No idea," I said, rocking gently in the chair deep in thought. Then an idea bubbled to the surface. I leaned forward and wiggled my fingers in the air. "Could it be that simple?"

"What?"

I typed ProjectOrg2020 and hit the enter key. The computer opened immediately.

"Wow, I said, staring at the screen. "Sometimes I even scare myself."

"You got in?" he said, coming around the desk to look over my shoulder. "How the heck did you come up with that?"

"Lucky guess," I said, studying the collection of icons on the main page. I glanced over my shoulder. "What do you think? Should we poke around for a while?"

"Why stop now?" the Chief said, pulling a chair next to mine and sitting down. "Let's start with his email."

"Just like that?" I said, puzzled.

"What?"

"No mind your own business, Suzy? No reprimand?"

"You can thank my wife for that."

"I'm going to need a little more, Chief."

"We were talking about you the other night. I was going on about how relentless you can be."

"Gee, thanks, Chief," I said, scowling at him.

"No, I was saying it in a good way. You know, about how it was one of your strengths, but often uncontrollable. And she said if a guy got arrested a dozen times for the

81

same crime, it would be logical to assume he might do it again."

"She compared me to a criminal?"

"Not at all," he said. "She was merely pointing out that repetition is usually a sign of a fixed behavior. Snooping is what you do. And then my wife said something that really resonated."

"I can't wait to hear it."

"She said if your inability to control your snooping didn't keep you up at night, why the hell should it keep me awake?"

"Smart woman," I said, then laughed. "So, you've decided to just go with the flow, huh?"

"Whenever I can," he said, then pointed at the monitor. "Email."

I clicked the icon and Peters' emails loaded.

"You want to sort on date or name?" I said, glancing over at him.

"Let's start with name first."

I did and the emails appeared in alphabetical order. I slowly scrolled down the page.

"You see any names you recognize?" I said.

"Not yet. Keep going."

I did. I made it all the way to the letter L before I stopped.

"Lacey," I said. "There's a bunch of emails between the two of them."

"What's the most recent date?" Chief Abrams said.

"Two weeks ago," I whispered.

"I thought she said they broke up two years ago."

"She did," I said, shaking my head. "Geez, I sure hope she's not involved in whatever this thing is."

"Keep going," the Chief said. "We'll circle back after we get through all the names."

I scrolled further down the page. Then I laughed when I saw the name.

"I don't believe it," I said. "Larry the Loser."

"Lamplighter? The attorney?"

"The one and only," I said. "What the heck was Larry the Loser doing for Peters?"

"Legal work," the Chief deadpanned as he leaned in close for a better look.

"Good one, Chief," I said, studying the subject line on the email. "It looks like Larry drafted Peters' will."

"Is the will attached to the email?"

"No, it's not," I said. "What do you think?"

"Open it," Chief Abrams said.

"Really? Aren't we crossing the line a bit?"

"Don't worry. If we get caught, I'll take the hit."

"Okay," I said with a shrug. "You're the cop."

I opened the email, and we spent a few minutes scrolling through it. The message contained a list of names, and I couldn't miss the fact that Lacey was included as one of the beneficiaries. Other names were listed including, I assumed, family members who had the same surname.

"That's weird," I said.

"There aren't any assets listed," the Chief said. "Where the heck is the will?"

"This reads like Larry was confirming some information before he drafted it. The last sentence says the distribution of assets will be listed as Schedule A and be revealed during the reading of the will after Peters' death." I glanced over my shoulder at him. "Have you ever seen a will that didn't include the assets?"

"No, it's a first for me," Chief Abrams said.

"What's a first, Chief?"

We both looked at the door where Detective Williams was standing with a dark stare etched in place.

"Hey, Detective Williams," I said, going for casual. "You've come just in time."

"Actually, I was just thinking I got here too late. What are you doing?"

"Uh, reading Peters' email at the moment," the Chief said.

"How the heck did you get into his computer?" the detective said, heading for the desk.

"We got lucky," I said with a shrug.

"Who gave you permission to be poking around in there?"

I glanced at the Chief then pointed at him.

"He did."

"Unbelievable," Detective Williams said, shaking his head. "Just to be on the safe side, turn the computer off. I'm still waiting for my warrant."

I did, then sat back, chagrined. He sat down across from me then nodded.

"Okay, talk me through it."

"Really?" I said, surprised by the lack of resistance I was getting from him. "Man, it must be my lucky day."

Chapter 9

I started working my way through a mug of hot chocolate as I watched Josie poke the fire before adding another log. Satisfied with her work, she stretched out on a couch and took a sip of wine. Preoccupied with our thoughts, we both remained silent staring into the fireplace.

"They've been in there a long time," I said eventually.

"They have," Josie said, nodding without taking her eyes off the fire. "It makes sense. I know I have a lot of questions."

"Do you think she's involved?"

"I don't know," she whispered after a long pause. She sat up and tucked her legs underneath her.

"She said their relationship ended a couple of years ago. But they've been emailing on a regular basis."

"I wouldn't read too much into that," Josie said, topping off her wine. "Maybe Peters was having a hard time cutting the cord."

"And she was humoring him?"

"Well, she did say the guy was pretty unstable. Maybe she was worried what he might do to himself if she cut him off completely."

"Or what he might do to her?" I said, raising an eyebrow.

"Hey, we're in the middle of nowhere surrounded by a pack of wolfdogs. Right about now, I'll believe anything."

We heard the back door open and the sound of someone stomping snow off their boots. Moments later, Rooster entered and headed straight for the fireplace.

"Are they still in there?" he said, warming his hands.

"Yeah," I said. "What have you been doing out there?"

"Shoveling a path from the house to the garage. And then I spotted the Utonagan."

"Akna's out there?" I said.

"She is," Rooster said. "But I couldn't get near her. She's pretty spooked. I was going to try to get her into one of the cages, but she wouldn't go near them."

"Smart dog," Josie said.

"Probably enjoying her newfound freedom," I said. "We should leave some food out for her."

"Yeah, good call," Josie said, heading for the kitchen. "I'll leave it on the back porch."

I focused on Rooster who also seemed preoccupied with his thoughts.

"Did you and Lacey get a chance to talk last night?"

"We did," Rooster said, nodding. "She's an interesting woman. Did you know she spent six months volunteering in Africa working with rescued elephants?"

"Yeah, I think I remember that coming up in her interview."

"Duh," he said, shaking his head. "Sorry. Dumb question."

"Does she seem like someone who could have...?"

"Killed Peters?" he said, then continued without hesitating. "No, I don't. You?"

"No. But we've been surprised before."

"We have," he said, nodding.

"I saw Peters' will," I said.

"Really?"

"Not the actual will. Just the list of beneficiaries and instructions about the reading of the will," I said. "Lacey's on the list."

"Geez, that's not necessarily good news," Rooster said.

"No. Let's hope whatever Peters is leaving her isn't enough to give her a reason to get rid of him."

"I'm sure the Chief and Detective Williams are exploring that possibility," he said. "Did you get the name of the lawyer who drafted the will?"

"Larry Lamplighter."

"Larry the Loser? Unbelievable. I guess bottom feeders of a feather flock together."

I laughed.

"I wonder how those two managed to connect," Rooster said, then noticed the look on my face. "What is it?"

"I'm wondering about something else," I said. "Like how to get invited to the reading of the will."

"Did you see your name on the list of beneficiaries?"

"No."

"Then I don't like your chances."

"Unless we're able to make an offer a certain beneficiary can't refuse."

"A certain beneficiary?" Rooster said with a frown. Then the penny dropped. "You're talking about the person Peters left this place to, right?"

"Nothing gets past you."

"You want to buy a hunting lodge?"

"Of course not," I said. "I just want to have a conversation about the possibility of buying it."

"That's interesting," he said. "It's not the worst idea you've ever had. But it's probably in the top ten."

"Funny."

"What on earth do you hope to find?" Rooster said.

"If we're trying to build a list of suspects, I can't think of a better place to start than by talking with the people who'll be inheriting whatever Peters decided to leave them."

"But you just said the contents of the will aren't included in the document," Rooster said.

"Maybe Peters was a talker," I said. "Maybe he told one or more of the beneficiaries what his plans were."

"Anything is possible," he said. "And you want Lacey to help you get invited to the reading?"

"I doubt if we'll be able to actually sit in on the reading," I said with a shrug. "But I don't see why we wouldn't be welcome at Lamplighter's office while all the beneficiaries are there."

"You think Lacey will be willing to play along?"

"My guess is she'll happy to do it," I said. "Especially if she thinks it will help clear her name."

"She has to be a suspect."

"Yeah," I said. "The ex-girlfriend who mysteriously shows up in the area right around the time the guy gets killed. A woman who's named in his will. I hate to say it, but I can make it work."

"She didn't do it," Rooster said, shaking his head.

"No, probably not," I said. "But the cops will have to keep her on the list until she comes up with a solid alibi."

"Does she have one?"

"I sure hope so," I said with a shrug.

We heard the office door open followed by footsteps. Moments later, Lacey appeared in the doorway and headed for the couch across from me. She sat down, a look of anger and confusion etched in place.

"They think I might have killed Jeremy," she said, brushing her hair back from her face.

"Did they accuse you?" I said.

"Not directly. But it was pretty hard to miss the direction they were going," she said. "I can't believe it."

"Did they tell you about the will?" I said.

"They did."

"What do you think Jeremy left you?" Rooster said.

"I have no idea," she said, her eyes pleading.

"What about all the emails?" I said.

"They were always initiated by Jeremy," she said. "I couldn't stop them. He was relentless."

"About wanting to get back together with you?" Rooster said.

"Yes. It wore me out."

"Did he go into what he was working on?" Rooster said.

"No, I refused to get into any sort of conversation that might reopen the door," she said. "I didn't want to encourage him. I did my best to deflect and remain neutral."

"Why didn't you tell him not to contact you? Or just ignore his emails?" I said.

"I was worried about him," Lacey said. "And I hoped we might be able to stay friends."

"Got it," I said. "Where did you leave it with the cops?"

"They said they'd be in touch if they have any more questions. Oh, I almost forgot. Would it be okay if I didn't come to the Inn for a few days? I'd like to examine the hybrids. And I really want to get a closer look at that litter of pups."

"That's a good idea," I said. "But you're going to need some help. You don't want to be doing that by yourself."

"I'll give her a hand," Rooster said, then had a thought. He looked over at Lacey. "You will be sedating them, right?"

"The two males, definitely," Lacey said. "We'll play it by ear with the others."

"Okay, count me in."

The office door opened, and Chief Abrams poked his head out.

"Hey, Suzy? You got a minute?" he called out.

"Be right there," I said, trying to push myself up off the couch. I failed miserably and shook my head. I glanced at Rooster. "I think I'm going to need a hand."

Rooster grabbed both of my hands and gently pulled me to my feet. I slowly made my way down the hall into the office. Detective Williams was sitting behind the desk.

"What's up?" I said, easing myself into a chair. I glanced back and forth at them then frowned. "Am I in trouble already?"

"Not at all," the Chief said with a laugh.

"We were wondering if you could do us a favor," Detective Williams said.

"I'll do my best. What do you need?"

"We'd like to enlist your snooping abilities," the Chief said.

"Since when?" I said, raising an eyebrow.

"We'd like you to research Peters' computer," Detective Williams said casually.

"I must have entered an alternative universe," I said, again glancing back and forth at the two cops. "You know, somehow broken through the space-time continuum."

"We're going to be busy working on other things the next few days," Detective Williams said, choosing his words carefully.

"Why don't you ask somebody you work with?" I said. "You must have lots of people looking for something to do this time of year."

"Well, given the fact there might be information on the computer about the wolfdogs, we thought you'd be the best person to handle it," the Chief said with a shrug. "You know, since we'd only have to circle back with you and Josie if we did find anything. It should save us some time."

"Yes, it's a timesaving strategy," Detective Williams said, nodding.

I studied the blank stares they were giving me and frowned.

"Nice try," I said. I focused on Chief Abrams. "What's going on, Chief?"

"Nothing's going on. We just need your help."

I stared off into space for several moments, then the penny dropped.

"You talked to my mother, didn't you?"

"Maybe," the Chief said, unable to make eye contact.

"She's worried I'm going to start traipsing around the countryside looking for Peters' killer, isn't she?"

"Maybe."

"Unbelievable."

"Suzy, it makes a lot of sense," the Chief said. "The last thing you need at the moment is too much excitement."

"It's an important part of the investigation," Detective Williams said, tossing in his two cents. "We need to get a good inventory of what's on that computer."

"And if I'm sitting in front of a computer screen, you won't have to worry about me getting in the way."

"We just want you to be safe," the Chief said.

"It'll be much better than trekking through the cold and snow," Detective Williams said.

"I can't argue with that," I said, shrugging. "What do you need?"

"We need all the stuff on his computer organized by category," Detective Williams said. "Friends and associates. What they were corresponding about. Money references. Research. Whatever makes sense."

"Okay," I said, nodding. "How long have I got?"

"Take all the time you need," the Chief said.

"A couple of days should be plenty," the detective said. "At least to get the ball rolling."

"What will you guys be doing in the meantime?"

"We have some people to talk to," Detective Williams said.

"Like Larry the Loser?" I said.

"He's definitely on the list," the Chief said.

"And I assume you'll be checking out what Lacey told you during her interview?"

"We will," Detective Williams said.

"She's a suspect, isn't she?" I said, again glancing back and forth at them.

"Let's call her a person of interest and leave it at that for now," Detective Williams said.

"Sure, sure," I said, nodding. Then I focused on the Chief. "You called my mother, didn't you?"

"I did. About an hour ago."

"Your phone works out here?"

"It does."

I thought about it then nodded.

"Well played, Chief."

"Yeah, I thought so."

Chapter 10

I was up early the next morning. I let the house dogs out to take care of business then made coffee and toasted an English muffin while I waited for it to brew. It didn't take long for the dogs to make their presence known at the back door, and I let them back in. All four were covered in snow.

"You guys were out there five minutes. How the heck did you manage that?" I said with a laugh. "Shake."

They did and I shook my head at the dusting of snow that flew off them and drifted down onto the tile floor. I toweled them off, gave them snacks then watched them head for the living room. I dragged the towel across the floor with my foot and tossed it into the hamper we kept near the door. I devoured the muffin, poured myself a cup of coffee then joined the dogs in the living room. They were already curled up in front of the fireplace. Chloe looked up at me expectantly.

"Not a chance," I said, laughing. "If you want a fire, you'll have to wait for Josie and Chef Claire to get up."

Chloe snorted then tucked herself close to Captain who was already sound asleep. I set my coffee down on an end table then fired up Peters' laptop. I grabbed a pen and pad of paper and sat down on the far end of the couch. Al and Dente, Chef Claire's Goldens, made a beeline for the couch and were soon battling for space. As I waited for them to get settled, I began jotting down several questions I was hoping to get answered.

Before I could make much progress, Josie entered the living room, yawning and stretching.

"Good morning. You're getting an early start. Coffee on?"

"It is," I said.

She headed to the fireplace and spent a few minutes saying hello to Captain and Chloe. Then she did the same with Al and Dente.

"You want a top up?" she said, heading for the kitchen.

"No, I'm good. Thanks." I said, opening Peters' email. "Hey, good morning."

Chef Claire was in the doorway, also in the process of trying to wake up.

"What time did you get home last night?" I said.

"It was pretty late. After we closed the dining room, we locked up and had an impromptu staff party in the lounge."

"I'm sorry I missed it."

"It won't be long," Chef Claire said. "How are you feeling?"

"I'm fine," I said, rubbing my stomach. "Just ready for this to be over. You going cross-country skiing today?"

"No, I'm taking the day off. I thought I'd spend it in front of the fire reading and playing with the dogs."

"Not the briar patch," Josie said, returning with two mugs of coffee. She handed one to Chef Claire then sipped hers. "I'm going to do the same thing."

"Nothing on your calendar?" I said.

"Not a thing," Josie said. "Did you find anything yet?"

"Just getting started," I said, jotting down a note.

"I can't believe Detective Williams asked for your help," Chef Claire said. "When it comes to your involvement, he's usually…"

"Snarky?"

"I was going to say guarded, but close enough."

I concentrated on the emails and was soon oblivious to my surroundings. I opened the one I'd read yesterday and started by making a list of the beneficiaries. There were five. Besides Lacey, they included Peters' wife, his brother, a woman named Clarissa, and a man who appeared to be a business associate of Peters. I closed the document and continued scrolling through the correspondence between

Peters and his lawyer. I paused when I noticed an email with Updated Will in the subject line. I read it with a frown then opened the attached document.

Josie noticed the puzzled look on my face.

"What's the matter?"

"I don't know," I said. "Something is bugging me. Maybe it's just the fact that Peters hired Larry to do his will. It seems strange."

Josie and Chef Claire both put their books down.

"Maybe they were buddies," Josie said.

"Yeah, maybe," I said. "But Larry the Loser isn't the sort of guy who has a lot of friends."

"I remember him from the restaurant," Chef Claire said. "He's really creepy. None of the servers want him sitting in their stations."

"He's always staring around the dining room," Josie said.

"Probably waiting for somebody to choke on a chicken bone so he can sue the restaurant," I said.

"Have you ever used him?" Chef Claire said.

"My mom hired him once to handle the contract for a piece of property she was buying. He was having trouble getting his business off the ground, so she decided to throw some work his way. But he completely screwed it up."

"What happened?" Chef Claire said.

"He put the wrong address in the contract. It didn't get noticed until my mom got a phone call from one of her friends wondering what the heck she was doing trying to buy their place. You know, since it wasn't actually for sale."

"How embarrassing for her," Josie said, laughing.

"Yeah, Larry almost blew the deal," I said. "That was the last time she tried to help him out."

"What kind of legal work does he do?" Chef Claire said.

"I think it's pretty much basic contract stuff," I said. "But he's always looking for a chance to take on personal injury lawsuits. Last year, he got a guy fifty thousand for a fall he took at Jackson's store."

"What happened to the guy?" Chef Claire said.

"He slipped on a grape," I said. "And guess who just happened to be in the store when it happened?"

"I'm gonna go with Larry the Loser for a thousand, Alex," Josie said.

"Bingo. And guess what was in Larry's shopping cart?"

"Grapes?"

"You're on fire today," I said, then focused on the computer screen.

I spent the next several minutes reviewing the email correspondence between Peters and the lawyer. I was about to move on when my neurons surged. I flinched, startling both Goldens who were still sprawled out next to me on the couch.

"Here we go," Josie said, glancing over at me.

"She's got the look," Chef Claire said with a grin. "That didn't take long."

"What have you got, Snoopmeister?" Josie said, setting her book down.

"I'm not sure. But something seems off," I said, studying the email I was reading. "What the heck is it?"

"Just let it marinate for a while," Josie said, then went back to her book.

I did.

I stared into the crackling fire and waited for some clarity to bubble to the surface. I rubbed my eyes and forced myself to relax. I reread the email then sighed loudly.

"You want some help?" Josie said, again putting her book down.

"Listen to this. It's the last email from Larry dealing with the will," I said, then read from the email. "Dear, Jeremy. Pursuant to our last conversation, I have made the minor edits to page seven. Attached is a PDF copy, and I have the original here in my office along with your asset inventory and instructions for their distribution at the time of your death. The edits are limited to spelling corrections and other minor cosmetic changes. I have deleted the previous page seven and updated the document with the new version. As such, there is no need for you to resign it. Simply delete the previous version and replace it with this one. Should you have any questions or need to discuss anything further, blah, blah, blah. Sincerely, Lawrence Lamplighter."

I glanced over at Josie who stared back at me and shrugged.

"What's bugging you about that? It sounds pretty straightforward," she said.

"I'm no lawyer," I said. "But shouldn't any updated version of a contract be signed again?"

"Maybe Peters didn't want to make the drive into town," Josie said. "Or he couldn't get Larry to come to him."

"Yeah, I guess I can make that work," I said, minimizing the email and scanning the other icons on the desktop screen.

"What are you looking for?" Josie said.

"Just checking to see if Peters didn't get around to deleting the earlier version," I said. "I'm looking for a folder named Personal or something like that."

"She's nothing if not thorough," Chef Claire said, then went back to her book.

"Probably not the word I would use."

"Shut it."

I continued studying the names of the icons on the screen then spotted something that piqued my curiosity.

"Here we go," I said, opening a folder titled Life Crap. I reviewed the list of documents contained in the folder then beamed at both of them. "Well, look at this."

"You found it?" Josie said.

"I did." I scrolled through the document and compared it to the updated version of the will the lawyer had attached to the email. "Larry didn't even bother changing the date. Why would he do that?"

"Lazy?" Chef Claire said.

"Or he didn't see the need since the changes were so minor," Josie said.

I studied the two identical signature pages then scrolled back to page seven in both documents. I noticed a handful of minor edits, all spelling corrections as the lawyer had referenced in his email. Then a deep frown emerged and remained fixed in place.

"What's the matter?" Josie said.

"Take a look," I said, turning the laptop so she could see the screen.

Josie approached the couch and sat down. Al opened one eye and stared at her as if daring her to ask him to move.

"Relax, Al," Josie said, rubbing the Golden's head. "What am I looking for?"

"Compare the pages," I said, my neurons on fire.

"Let me see," Chef Claire said, leaning over the back of the couch. "You're right. The signatures are identical. And they both have the same date."

"Yeah," I said. "They're definitely the same on both versions."

"I'm not picking anything up," Josie said.

"Look at the top of the page on both documents," I said, scrolling back and forth.

"They start with different text," Josie said.

"They do."

"But doesn't that make sense?" Chef Claire said. "The layout probably changed when he made the edits."

"No, I just looked at the edits Larry referenced in his email," I said, shaking my head. "They're very minor and wouldn't have changed the layout. And those edits didn't start until page seven."

"Maybe there were other changes earlier in the document," Chef Claire said.

"That's what I'm thinking," I said, scrolling back to the first page of both documents. Then I moved to page two. I studied them then flinched. Josie barely reacted.

"I was ready for that one," she said, studying the documents.

"You were on Flinch Alert?"

"I was."

"Unbelievable," I said, shaking my head as I compared the two versions.

"That I was ready for it?" Josie said, confused.

"No. I can't believe Lamplighter had the cojones to pull this off," I said, pointing at the list of people named in the will. "The beneficiaries start at the bottom of page one and continue on the next. This is amazing."

"He added himself as a beneficiary?" Josie said, stunned.

"It certainly looks like it," I said.

"But how could Peters not pick that up?" Chef Claire said.

"The guy named his personal folder, Life Crap," I said. "My guess is Peters hated it when life got in the way of his research. Maybe Larry rolled the dice and figured Peters wouldn't spend much time looking at it."

"And his email referenced the minor edits on page seven," Josie said. "Peters probably took a quick look at them and didn't even bother reviewing the rest of the document."

"It's actually quite brilliant," Chef Claire said, then caught the looks we were giving her. "You know, from a criminal standpoint."

"Yeah," I said, giving it some thought. "Especially if Peters and Larry were the only two who knew what was actually in the will."

"And since Peters would be dead when the will was read, who would ever know?" Chef Claire said.

"It is pretty clever," I said. Then my neurons surged, and I scrolled back to the signature page. "Hang on."

"What?" Josie said, staring at the screen.

"There's a witness listed on the signature page," I said, studying the name. "Althea Jones. She was Larry's assistant."

"Was?" Josie said.

"Althea left town a few months ago," I said.

"I did not know that," Josie said.

"She moved somewhere out west."

"You think she might be involved?"

"Hang on. Just give me a sec," I said, studying the date of the contract and the email Larry had sent Peters. "There's a two-month gap between the date of the will and the email where Larry mentions the edited one. I don't think Althea left the area until after the date on the email."

"Maybe she's getting a cut," Josie said.

"It's certainly possible," I said.

"That should be easy enough to check," Chef Claire said.

"Yeah, I'll ask the Chief tonight to track her down," I said. "He confirmed he's coming to family dinner. That reminds me. Whose turn is it to cook?"

"Mine," Josie said. "How does beef bourguignon with a sweet potato-celeriac mash sound?"

"Like music to my ears," I said, not looking up from the document.

"Would you mind swinging by the restaurant and grabbing a loaf of the rustic Italian?" Josie said to Chef Claire. "On second thought, you might want to get two."

"No problem," Chef Claire said, then focused on me. "If this gets out, isn't it the end of Larry's legal career?"

"You mean when it gets out, right?" I said. "Yeah, he'll be toast. But that could end up being the least of his problems."

"You think he might have killed Peters?" Josie said.

"Well, the guy went to all the trouble of adding himself as a beneficiary. And the only way the will gets read is if Peters is dead."

"Can't argue with your logic," Josie said with a shrug. "That must mean Larry probably also modified how Peters' assets were going to be distributed."

"It does," I said. "I wonder what he gave himself."

"We'll know after the will gets read," Josie said.

"Yeah, but I'd love to hear it *while* it's being read," I said.

"But as soon as the cops hear what Larry's been up to, that's going to postpone the reading of the will," Chef Claire said.

"Not necessarily," I said, grinning as I glanced back and forth at them.

"This oughta be good," Josie said.

"Oh, it's good," I said, my neurons on full-tilt. "All we need is our two cop buddies willing to go along with it and a sympathetic judge."

Josie thought about my comment then the penny dropped.

"Judge Thompson, right?"

"Nothing gets past you."

"That's brilliant."

"Aren't you sweet."

Chapter 11

I pulled the Chief by his shirtsleeve as soon as he got his coat off and nodded for him to follow me into the living room. I poured him a glass of wine and sat down across from him. He took a sip, nodded his approval then smiled when he saw the look on my face.

"How was your day?" he said, going for coy.

"Is it that obvious?"

"If there's one thing I know, it's when your brain has been working overtime," he said, taking another sip. "What have you got?"

"Larry the Loser added himself as a beneficiary to Peters' will."

"What?" he said, stunned.

I spent a few minutes telling him the story, and he listened closely, alternating sips of wine with nods and the occasional head shake. When I finished, I sat back and waited for questions.

"I always knew the guy was a bottom feeder, but this is a new low. Even for him," the Chief said, holding his glass out so I could top it off.

"Did you get a chance to talk to him?"

"No, he's been out of town and just got back today. Detective Williams and I are meeting with him in the morning. You mentioned there was a witness."

"Yes. Althea Jones."

"I remember her. She left town a few months ago."

"She did."

"Let me give Detective Williams a call," he said, reaching for his phone. "Hey. It's Chief Abrams…Yeah, I'm good. Sorry to bother you, but we've had a bit of a breakthrough…She did…Yeah, it was fast, wasn't it? Actually, Suzy's right here. You want to talk to her?"

"Invite him to dinner," I said.

"Good idea," the Chief said. "What are we having?"

"Beef bourguignon."

"Great. With the rustic Italian?"

"Of course."

"Suzy just invited you to dinner," the Chief said into the phone. "No, not the restaurant. At her place. Trust me, you don't want to miss it…That's great. We'll be here. Hang on. Before you go, I was wondering if you could run a name for us…Althea Jones. Formerly of Clay Bay, but now living somewhere out west. I think she was heading to Colorado…Okay, we'll see you in a bit." The Chief ended the call. "He's on his way."

"Perfect," I said, then spotted my mother and Paulie heading for us. "Hey, Mom. You look great. Nice outfit. Is that new?"

"Rhetorical, right?" Paulie said, grinning at me.

"Oh, hush," my mother said, squeezing his arm before sitting down.

"Did I get that right?" Paulie said.

"You did," I said, laughing. "Well played."

"I spent yesterday in Montreal shopping for my new granddaughter. But I decided I might as well pick something up for myself while I was there."

"It looks great," I said. "But if you keep buying crap for her, we're going to have to build an addition to hold it all."

"Crap?"

"Figure of speech, Mom. That was very sweet of you."

"Thank you, darling," she said, pouring wine for both of them. "I assume you spent the day exploring Peters' computer?"

"I did," I said, raising an eyebrow at her. "And I can't help but get the feeling you're doing everything you can to control my behavior."

"Aren't you enjoying your assignment?" she said.

"I am. But that's not the point. I don't need you to babysit me."

"Well, we'll just have to disagree about that, darling," she said, draping a leg over her knee. "Have you found anything yet?"

"Larry Lamplighter was Peters' lawyer."

"Geez," my mother grunted. "They're perfect for each other."

"And Larry added himself as a beneficiary to the guy's will."

"Are you joking?" my mother said.

"Nope," I said, then focused on Paulie. "You used to be a criminal, right?"

"Vicious and unfounded rumors," Paulie said with a crocodile smile.

Chief Abrams snorted.

"Please, darling. Don't start. Why on earth would you bring that up?"

"I'm just wondering if Paulie ever came across a situation like this."

"You mean, a lawyer falsifying documents?" Paulie said.

"Yeah."

"Sure," he said with a shrug. "All the time. But never without the client's permission."

"That's what I figured," I said, nodding. "Larry must have been convinced Peters would never find out."

"By making sure he was dead?" Paulie said.

"The thought has crossed my mind. What would you have done if you discovered your lawyer had tried to pull something like that on you?"

"I'll refrain from comment," Paulie said, glancing at the Chief. "But I'm sure you can use your imagination."

"What's he getting from Peters' estate?" my mother said.

"We don't know yet," I said. "The distribution of assets isn't going public until the reading of the will."

"I didn't think Larry had it in him to pull something like this off," my mother said. "But I'm sure it beats staging 'slip and sue' accidents."

Josie entered the room and topped off her wine glass.

"Dinner will be ready in five minutes," she said.

"It'll hold, right?" I said. "I just invited Detective Williams, and he's on his way."

"Not a problem," she said. "I'll set another place."

Fifteen minutes later, we were all sitting at the dining room table. Josie spooned a generous portion of the bourguignon into each bowl then topped them off with the sweet potato-celeriac mash. Chef Claire passed around a cutting board of the sliced Italian rustic then we all went to work on our dinners.

"Great job," I said, finally pausing long enough to speak.

"Thanks," Josie said, dipping a piece of bread into the red-wine gravy.

"The mash is wonderful, dear," my mother said.

"What else is in it besides sweet potato?" Detective Williams said.

"Celeriac," Josie said.

"I'm picking up celery," he said.

"It's from the celery family," Chef Claire said. "It grows as a bulb. Like a turnip. It's good raw, too."

"I'll take your word for it," Detective Williams said. "I'm not big on raw vegetables." His phone buzzed, and he wiped his mouth before getting to his feet. "Sorry, but I need to take this."

He headed into the living room, and the rest of us resumed eating and chatting about nothing. A few minutes later, Detective Williams returned and sat down with a frown on his face.

"Bad news?" the Chief said.

"Yeah, it was," he said, toying with his food as he stared off at the far wall. "Surprising news to say the least."

"Well, don't keep us in suspense," I said, leaning forward.

"Althea Jones was killed in a car crash," the detective said. "Her car went off the side of a mountain. A thousand feet. They found her in a ravine. Apparently, she'd been there awhile."

"Single car crash?" the Chief said.

"Yeah."

"The poor woman," I said. "Are the cops calling it accidental?"

"They don't have much choice," Detective Williams said.

"Why's that?" Josie said, helping herself to seconds.

"Have you ever seen a car after a thousand-foot drop?" Detective Williams said. "Not to mention the person who was in it."

"Got it," Josie said with a frown. "Geez. That's awful. I liked Althea."

"She came into the restaurant just before she left town," Chef Claire said.

"Who was she with?" I said.

"Larry the Loser," Chef Claire said. "They said it was her going away dinner."

"How did they seem?" the Chief said.

Chef Claire gave it some thought then shook her head.

"Nothing stood out," she said. "Just two people having dinner."

"So, now it's just Larry's word," Chief Abrams said.

"How convenient for him," I said, grabbing a piece of bread and dredging it through the last of the gravy. "What time are you meeting with him in the morning?"

"Ten," the Chief said, then caught the look on my face. "What is it?"

"Nothing," I said, avoiding the look my mother was giving me. "Is it my turn to do the dishes?"

"No, it's mine," Chef Claire said.

"Let me give you a hand, dear," my mother said.

"Thanks, Mrs. C. Why don't you guys head into the living room? We'll have coffee and dessert in there."

"Where are the bruisers?" Josie said.

"They're downstairs in the game room," Chef Claire said. "They'll be fine until we finish."

I got up and slowly made my way to a couch. The Chief watched me work my way into a sitting position with a grin then sat down next to me.

"Not a word," I said, making a face at him.

"I wouldn't think of it," he said, laughing. "You look great."

"I feel like a beached whale," I said, holding my stomach. "And I ate too much."

"Well, you are eating for two and a half."

"Funny," I said, gently punching him on the shoulder.

"Okay," Detective Williams said. "Now that we have a little privacy, why don't you tell me all about the breakthrough you had today?"

I glanced at the Chief, and he motioned for me to tell the story.

"Larry the Loser added himself as a beneficiary to Peters' will."

Detective Williams' expression morphed into a deer in the highlights look. He quickly recovered and stared at me.

"Talk to me, Suzy."

I did.

When I finished, he took a sip of Limoncello and exhaled loudly.

"Wow."

"That's all you got?" I said, laughing.

"Yeah," he said, grinning at me. "I'm gonna need a minute. If Peters had actually deleted the other version of the will, we never would have known."

"We might have been able to guess what he did," I said. "But I doubt if we could ever prove it."

"Did you find a copy of how his assets were going to be distributed?" Detective Williams said.

"No," I said. "My guess is Larry has the only copy."

"Which means he had free reign to change it as he saw fit," Detective Williams said. "Talk about a game changer. What do you think, Chief?"

"We'll know more tomorrow after we talk to him," he said.

I frowned but remained silent. They both noticed the look on my face, and the Chief sat back in his chair studying me closely.

"Let's hear it," he said.

"I'd wait. But that's just me."

"You'd wait to talk to him?" Detective Williams said.

"No, I'd definitely talk to him," I said. "But I wouldn't let on you know what he did. Or about what happened to Althea."

"The reading of the will," Chief Abrams said.

"Exactly," I said. "I'd let it proceed and see how Larry plays it."

"I'm willing to bet the beneficiaries are going to be very surprised when they hear the news," Detective Williams said. "Yeah, I like it. Good call, Suzy."

"Thanks. I can't wait to hear what Larry has to say for himself," I said, glancing back and forth at them with a coy smile.

"*You* can't wait?" the Chief said.

"I think we should listen in when the will is read," I said.

"We?" Detective Williams said.

"You can't cut me out now, Detective Williams," I said, beaming at him. "We're just getting started."

"We'll need a judge to sign off on the surveillance," the Chief said. "But given what we've got, that shouldn't be a problem."

"And I have the perfect judge to use," I said.

They both focused on me and waited.

"Judge Thompson."

"Thompson?" Detective Williams said. "Suzy, the guy has a reputation for being incredibly tough on lawyers and cops."

"Yes, he does," I said. "But I'm willing to bet he's crossed paths with Larry in the past. If he has, I seriously doubt he's a fan."

"I'm sure he's not," the Chief said. "But still, Thompson sets a high bar for stuff like this."

"If Judge Thompson thinks he can get a corrupt lawyer disbarred, he'll go along," I said. "Not to mention the possibility Larry might get convicted of murder."

"Are you sure we're talking about the same Judge Thompson?" Detective Williams said.

"I am," I said. "I've dealt with him many times."

"You've been in front of the judge?" Detective William said, confused.

"I moonlight as a court reporter," I deadpanned.

The Chief laughed and sipped his Limoncello.

"Why do I think I'm about to hear a dog story?" he said.

"The judge and his wife breed poodles. Whenever they travel, they always board their dogs with us. And you'll never guess the name of the vet who works with their dogs exclusively."

"They drive their puppies to the Inn?" the Chief said.

"No, Josie and I go to them," I said with a shrug. "We have a great relationship with the Thompsons."

122

"Okay," Detective Williams said. "I guess it can't hurt to take you along. I'll give his office a call in the morning."

"Larry is probably going to want to do the reading as soon as possible," I said. "I wonder what he's giving himself from Peters' estate."

"Maybe he'll tip his hand in the morning," Chief Abrams said.

"No offense, but I doubt if he's going to tell the cops anything," I said. "But he might open up to an old classmate."

"You went to school with the guy?" Detective Williams said.

"I did."

"And you want to swing by his office first thing in the morning, right?" the Chief said.

"I thought I might."

"For what reason?" Detective Williams said.

"I'll think of something."

Chapter 12

Larry Lamplighter, aka the Loser, got his nickname early in life. All throughout school, he'd been one of those kids who never quite fit in, was a half-step behind in most conversations, and, for reasons unknown to the rest of us, had an extremely high opinion of himself. Given Clay Bay's small size, our paths crossed regularly, but we never hung out. In fact, Larry rarely hung out with anybody. It wasn't that his classmates disliked him; Larry was basically ignored. As such, he'd spent his childhood on the periphery, relegated to the role of observer rather than participant.

I slowly climbed the front steps that led to the office he operated out of his house not far from downtown. I entered and glanced around the reception area then spotted a bell sitting on top of an empty desk. I tapped it and took another look around as I waited. The area had the antiseptic feel of a doctor's waiting room, and I was just about to sit down when Larry Lamplighter wandered down the hall toward me. He grinned when he saw me and extended his hand.

"Suzy Chandler," he said, pumping my hand several times before letting go and spreading his arms wide. "Welcome to my world."

"Hi, Larry. It's been a long time. How are you doing?"

"Great. Just great," he said, giving me the once-over. "Look at you. You're not going to pop in my office, are you?" Then he laughed hard at his own joke.

"Pop?"

"You know, go into labor."

"Got it. No, that's not on the list," I said, forcing a smile.

"Good. I'd hate to have to charge you for cleaning the place."

"Or sue me, right?"

"Good one," he said. "You always were one of the funny ones. So, what can I do for you?"

"I need a little legal advice."

"Then you have definitely come to the right place."

"Where's your receptionist?"

"Paralegal-receptionist," he said, correcting me. "I haven't got around to replacing Althea yet. I need to get on that. I still can't believe she left me."

"Left you?"

"Figure of speech," Larry said with a shrug. "C'mon, follow me. I think you'll like what I've done with the office."

I followed him into a large office and glanced around at the furnishings. Early-roadside-motel was the best description I could come up with, and I remained standing until he waved me into a chair on the other side of his desk. Hanging on the wall behind his desk were several photos, most of which were panoramic shots of the Thousand Islands. But one caught my attention, and I leaned forward to get a better look.

"Is that our high school graduation picture?" I said, surprised.

"It is," he said, beaming at it. "Those were good times, huh?"

"Yeah," I said, shaking my head when I spotted my goofy smile staring back at me. "Wow. I haven't seen that picture in years."

"Remember that time we took your mom's pontoon boat over to the Lake of the Isles?"

"Which time?" I said, trying to isolate the event from several possibilities.

"Junior year. Summer. August, I think," he said, giving it some serious thought. "Now that was a party. We must have had thirty people on that boat."

"Sure, sure," I said, frowning as my memory bank came up empty. Not the party, but the fact that Larry had been there.

"Does your mom still have it?"

"No, she still has a pontoon boat, but she's upgraded a few times since then."

"How's she doing?"

"She's great."

"Glad to hear it. Is she still holding a grudge for the time I messed up that contract?"

"My mother doesn't really hold grudges."

"Good to know."

"She tends to strangle them," I whispered.

"What?"

"Nothing."

"Okay, we should probably get started," he said, glancing at his watch. "I have a ten o'clock. But if we don't have time to finish, we'll get something on the old calendar, huh?"

"This shouldn't take long. I just need to bounce a few ideas off you."

"Lay it on me," he said, leaning forward with his elbows on the desk.

"I'm thinking about setting up a trust for my daughter. And I don't have a clue where to start."

"That's why they make lawyers," he said, spreading his hands to emphasize his point. "What sort of trust are you thinking about?"

"Something safe that I can add to on a regular basis, but won't be accessible until she's twenty-one. Or maybe eighteen."

"Piece of cake," he said. "And you'll need someone to manage it. You know, a certified financial planner. Or a lawyer with a finance background. Yeah, I can definitely help you with that."

"I didn't know you also handled financials," I said, tossing my line into the water.

"Actually, I'm just getting into it," he said.

"Really?"

"Yeah, I recently fell into an opportunity and decided to focus on it," he said. "Between you and me, it's where the money is."

"It's gotta be easier than suing business owners, right?"

"Huh? Oh, yeah. Good one."

I reached into my bag and removed a large Ziploc. I held it out to him.

"Grape?"

"Thanks," he said, frowning. "I'll pass."

"So, how does the whole trust thing work?" I said, tossing a couple grapes into my mouth.

"Well, we draw up a contract that outlines the parameters of how you want it to work. Then we get it registered. And your trustee makes sure all the filings and tax documents are submitted on time. You can have as much or as little day to day control over the trust as you want. Personally, I'd delegate all that to the trustee. You know, so you don't have to worry about stuff like that."

"How long does it take to set up?" I said.

"Not long," he said. "In fact, I should be able to get it going before I leave."

"You're leaving?"

"Yeah, it's time for these old bones to be in the sun and sand," he said. He pressed the tips of his fingers together and rocked gently in his chair. "I just can't take these winters."

"I get that," I said, nodding. "But if you're leaving the area, won't that be a problem?"

"For the trust?" he said, frowning. "Not at all. That's why they give us email and cellphones, right?"

"Yeah, I suppose you're right. So, where are you going?"

"I haven't decided," he said. "Someplace without snow and ice."

"And extradition," I whispered.

"What?"

"Nothing."

"Look, why don't you give me a few days to pull some stuff together and then we'll sit down and knock it out. How does Friday work for you?"

"As long as I'm not in the hospital."

"Hospital?" he said, frowning. Then the penny dropped. "Oh, right. Duh."

I slowly worked my way out of my chair and extended my hand.

"Thanks, Larry. I appreciate your help."

"Hey, that's why I'm here, right? It was nice seeing you, Suzy. I'll be in touch."

We both headed out of the office. As we walked down the hall, I spotted a photo of Larry standing next to Althea on a dock.

"Where was that taken?" I said, coming to a stop and taking a closer look at it.

"Downriver somewhere," he said. "I don't really remember."

"You both look happy."

"Yeah, we were," he said, staring at the photo.

"Why did Althea leave?"

"She just wanted more."

"From life?" I said, glancing at him.

"That's what she said. But I think the real reason was she wanted more than me."

"Ouch," I whispered.

"Yeah," he said. "Ouch indeed."

The front door opened, and Chief Abrams and Detective Williams entered. They both waved then removed their coats.

"My ten o'clock," Larry said, heading toward them.

"Cops in the morning, lawyers take warning," I said, following him. "Good morning, gentlemen."

"Hi, Suzy," the Chief said, then shook hands with the lawyer. "How are you doing, Larry?"

"I'm good, Chief."

"This is Detective Williams from the state police," the Chief said.

"It's nice to meet you, Detective. You sounded very official on the phone yesterday, Chief. What do you need to talk about?"

"Dr. Jeremy Peters," the Chief said without ceremony.

"Peters? Yeah, sure. I know Jeremy. What did he do?"

"You haven't heard?" Detective Williams said.

"I've been out of town," Larry said. "What happened? DUI? I hear the guy loves his wine."

"No. He's dead," Detective Williams said.

Larry the Loser visibly flinched and his eyes narrowed. I studied his face closely, but it gave nothing away.

"Jeremy's dead?" the lawyer whispered. "What happened?"

"He was hit in the back of the head with a blunt object," the Chief said. "Probably a chunk of firewood."

"Where?"

"Out at Cabot Lodge," the Chief said. "Are you familiar with the place?"

"Only on paper," Larry said with a shrug. Then he caught the look both cops were giving him and continued. "I handled Jeremy's will. And the lodge is listed as one of his assets."

"You said you've been out of town," Detective Williams said. "Can I ask where you were?"

"In Colorado."

"Skiing?" the Chief said.

Larry stared at the Chief, started to speak then stopped. Eventually, he continued.

"I went to Colorado to track down my former assistant," the lawyer said softly.

"Althea, right?" the Chief said.

"Yeah. We didn't depart on good terms, and I went out there to see if there was a chance I could talk her into coming back."

"How did that go?" the Chief said.

"I couldn't find her," Larry said. "It turned out the address she gave me was bogus. I guess she was telling the truth when she said she didn't want to see me anymore."

"Did you talk to the cops while you were out there?" Detective Williams said. "Maybe file a missing person report?"

"Why would I do that?" Larry said, his voice rising a notch. "It was, and still is, pretty clear she just doesn't want to talk to me."

Detective Williams glanced at me, and I nodded I understood it was time for me to take my leave.

"Maybe we should continue this conversation in your office," Detective Williams said.

"I need to run," I said, pulling on my coat. "Thanks for your help, Larry."

"Yeah, no problem," the lawyer said, obviously preoccupied with other thoughts. "I'll give you a call."

I headed for the door but stopped when Chief Abrams called after me.

"Suzy, you got a sec?"

"Sure, Chief. What's up?"

"I need to talk with you about using your place in Cayman," he said, seamlessly transitioning into his cover story.

"Oh, good. You guys decided to go down."

"You two go on ahead," the Chief said to Detective Williams. "I'll be there in a minute."

We watched the detective and lawyer walk down the hall. When they were out of earshot, the Chief sat down and motioned for me to do the same. Not wanting to deal with getting in and out of a chair, I stayed on my feet.

"What did he have to say for himself?" he said.

"He said he's leaving the area. For sun and sand."

"Interesting," the Chief said. "Take the money and run, huh?"

"I guess," I said, frowning. "But he seemed genuinely surprised about the news that Peters was dead."

"He's a lawyer," the Chief said. "He's probably used to hiding his real feelings. Or flat-out lying to our face."

"Yeah, I get that. But genuine shock is pretty hard to fake."

"Maybe. And he was in Colorado right around the time the woman's car went off a cliff."

"It seems too easy."

"Sometimes, it is that easy," he said.

"I suppose you're right."

"What else did he have to say?" the Chief said.

"He's branching out into financial services," I said. "Trustee services. Financial management. Stuff like that. He said he recently got an opportunity to make the transition."

"By writing himself into Peters' will," the Chief said.

"Yeah, I suppose," I said softly, deep in thought.

"You're not going to start overthinking this thing, are you?"

"Rhetorical, right?"

"Silly me," he said, getting to his feet. "I need to get back there. If you're willing to buy us lunch, we'll meet you at C's after we finish up."

"You got it."

"What's the special today?"

"I'm not sure. Does it matter?"

"It never has before."

Chapter 13

Judge Jeremiah Thompson was a vibrant guy somewhere in his late fifties with piercing blue eyes that could bring criminals and their lawyers to their knees. A man with a bite far worse than his bark, he wasn't shy about using the power of the bench to command order in his courtroom and keep the wheels of justice turning. And the wrath he showed on a regular basis for those he considered unruly or unprepared wasn't confined to defendants and their defense teams. He was as tough on prosecutors and law enforcement officials who came before him. As such, while feared and disliked by many, he commanded a level of respect that was the envy of most people who worked in and around the district courthouse.

We were escorted into his office by his assistant, and he immediately got out of his chair and beamed at me.

"Suzy Chandler," he said, giving me a hug. "Look at you. When's your due date?"

"I've got a few weeks to go," I said, patting my belly.

"Well, you look fantastic. By the way, nice work smoking out that corrupt FBI agent who was smuggling people across the River. Well done."

"Oh, you heard about that?" I said, surprised.

"I hear everything," he said as a simple statement of fact.

"You're looking good, Judge."

"Oh, knock that judge crap off," he said, waving my comment away. "Call me Jeremiah." Then he gave both cops the once-over. "But you two can call me, Judge Thompson."

"How are you, Judge Thompson?" Detective Williams said.

The judge's eyes narrowed as he studied the detective.

"Williams, right? You're with the staties," Judge Thompson said.

"Yes, sir."

"You testified in front of me about a year ago," the judge said, staring off momentarily. "Give me a sec. I'll remember. The Bobby Talbot case, right?"

"You've got a good memory, Your Honor," Detective Williams said.

"It's a little hard to forget lowlifes like Talbot. Yeah, I remember you. You did a good job. Stuck to the facts. Laid it all out in a way that was easy for the jury to follow. Yeah, I remember. You've got a nice Joe Friday quality I always appreciate."

"Thank you, sir."

"And you're Chief Abrams, right?" the judge said, extending his hand.

"I am. It's nice to finally meet you, Judge Thompson."

"Likewise," the judge said, nodding. "You run a tight ship down there. I hear good things about you. So, what can I do for you?"

"Well, you see, sir-" Detective Williams said.

"Hang on a sec," the judge said, focusing on me. "We've got a new litter coming soon. Make sure you let Josie know we're going to need her to stop by in a couple of weeks."

"Will do," I said. "Princess is having another litter?"

"Yeah," the judge said, nodding. "This will be her last one. Should be quite a collection. We mated her with a male who finished third in Best of Breed at nationals last year." He turned to the two cops. "My wife and I breed poodles."

"Nice," the Chief said.

"Smartest dogs on the planet," he said. "Smarter than most of the criminals who end up in front of me. And probably half the lawyers, too."

"Do you show them?" Detective Williams said.

"Nah," the judge said, shaking his head. "We leave that to other people. I prefer to let our dogs be dogs. As long as they don't run off or crap in the house, I'm a happy guy." He beamed at me. "Am I right or am I right?"

"Can't argue with your logic, Jeremiah," I said, laughing. "I'll let Josie know."

"Thanks. It'll be good to see her. How's she doing?"

"She's great."

"Good," he said, then sat down behind his desk and focused on Detective Williams. "You were saying?"

"We're here to request a surveillance warrant."

"I see," he said, nodding. "You got a good reason?"

"We think so, Your Honor," Detective Williams said.

"The last guy who got a warrant out of me because he *thought* he had a good reason was…well, never."

"I understand, sir," Detective William said, quickly backpedaling. "Let me rephrase. We're sure we have more than enough to justify a surveillance warrant."

"Much better," the judge said. "Continue."

"We've uncovered a corrupt lawyer."

"Geez, Detective," the judge said, frowning. "I do that on a daily basis before lunch. C'mon, get to it. Who are we talking about?"

"Larry Lamplighter."

"Lamplighter?" Judge Thompson said as a wide grin emerged. "Now, you're talking. I've been looking for a way to bury that bottom feeder for years. What did he do?"

"He wrote himself into a client's will as a beneficiary," Detective Williams said.

Judge Thompson burst into extended laughter. His eyes watered and he wiped them with a tissue before exhaling loudly.

"Beautiful," the judge said. "That's just frigging beautiful."

"We've never seen anything quite like it," Detective Williams said.

"How the heck did he think he was going to get away with that?" the judge said.

"Both the client and the individual who witnessed the signing of the will are dead," Detective Williams said.

Judge Thompson's eyes narrowed.

"And you think Lamplighter killed them?"

"It's a distinct possibility," Chief Abrams said.

"Who was the client?"

"Dr. Jeremy Peters," Detective Williams said.

"Doesn't ring a bell," the judge said, gently rocking in his chair. "What do you want the warrant for?"

"We'd like to listen in when the will is read," the detective said. "The distribution of Peters' assets isn't outlined in the will. We think it's going to be a major surprise for all the beneficiaries."

"And you want to see if somebody tips their hand?"

"Yes, Your Honor," Detective Williams said. "And we're hoping to make some sense of what the heck is going on."

"Lamplighter. A murderer? He never struck me as the type. Sleazeball, sure. But a murderer?"

"Our guess is there's a lot of money that's about to change hands," Chief Abrams said.

"Probably a good guess," the judge said, nodding. "What did this guy Peters do?"

"He was a genetic engineer," Detective Williams said. "And he did a lot of research."

"Is there money in that?" the judge said.

"If there is, we don't have a clue how he made it," Chief Abrams said. "There are a lot of questions and loose ends we need to deal with."

"And you think listening in on the reading is going to help?"

"We do, sir," Detective Williams said.

"When's the reading?"

"We met with Lamplighter yesterday. And he said he was going to set it up soon," Detective Williams said.

"After that, he said he plans on leaving the area," Chief Abrams said.

"Take the money and run?" the judge said.

"That's what it looks like," the Chief said. "Assuming he can duck murder charges."

Judge Thompson again stared off, deep in thought. Then he focused on me.

"How the heck did you get sucked up in this thing?"

"Peters has been breeding wolves with dogs," I said. "Creating hybrids. It was one of his research interests."

"That's despicable," Judge Thompson said, shaking his head. "How many did he have?"

"We found about twenty," I said. "At least three, maybe four generations. We're still not sure what percentage of wolf the offspring have. He's been using two purebred males."

"What's he been breeding them with?" the judge said.

"Utonagans, primarily," I said. "You familiar with the breed?"

"They're the ones that were crossbred to look like wolves but act like dogs?"

"That's them," I said.

"I just read a story the other day about some folks who thought one of those hybrids would make a great family dog."

"Big mistake," I said, shaking my head.

"Yeah," the judge said. "They don't get much bigger. Some people shouldn't be allowed to have kids."

"What happened?" I said.

"The hybrid killed their four-year-old."

"Geez," I grunted.

"What are you going to do with them?" the judge said.

"Long-term, we're not sure," I said. "But for now, we're keeping a close eye on them. And they're caged."

"At the Doggy Inn?" he said, raising an eyebrow at me.

"No, they're out in the woods at a hunting lodge Peters somehow came into possession of," I said. "We've got a new vet running our animal shelter. She's staying there until we figure something out."

The judge studied my face closely then motioned for me to continue.

"You're holding something back," he said. "What is it?"

"Our new vet used to be Peters' girlfriend," I said softly. "And she's also named in his will."

"Wow. How about that?" he said, pursing his lips. "It looks like you guys caught a juicy one."

"Yes, we did," Detective Williams said. "What do you think about the warrant, Your Honor?"

"Oh, you'll get a warrant," Judge Thompson said. "I just wish I could be there to listen in."

"I'm sure that can be arranged," Detective Williams said.

"I was joking, Detective. But I will want to hear the recording."

The judge got out of his chair and pulled his robe on.

"Stop back in a couple of hours," he said. "I'll have my assistant pull something together. She'll have it at her desk."

"Thank you, Judge Thompson."

"Lamplighter," he said, shaking his head as he left the office through a side door.

Chapter 14

I put the SUV in park and slowly climbed out. My right foot landed in three inches of slush covered by skim ice, and I grimaced expecting the worst. But it wasn't deep enough to cover my boots and I relaxed. I made my way to the back of the vehicle and opened the hatch.

"Crunchy slush," Josie said, shaking her head as she looked down at her feet. "My favorite."

"Yeah, it's a mess," I said, waving to Rooster who was making his way toward us. "But don't worry. In a few weeks, you'll have something even better to deal with."

"Rain and mud," Josie said, then gave Rooster a hug. "How's it going?"

"Not bad," Rooster said, grabbing the three bags of groceries. "The nightlife will never kill you, but I've been sleeping like a baby."

We followed him up the back steps, and I paused when I reached the porch to take a look at the row of cages where most of the animals were warily staring up at us.

"How are they doing?" I said.

"Apart from being caged up, they're fine," Rooster said. "But you have to keep a close eye on the two wolves.

Most of the time they're cautious and keep their distance. But if you get too close, they're not shy about letting you know."

"The poor things," I said.

"You come up with any ideas about what to do with them?" Rooster said.

"Not yet."

"There aren't a lot of options," Josie said, holding the door open for us.

"We've got a little surprise for you," Rooster said, stomping slush off his boots.

"French onion soup?" Josie said.

"What?"

"I've been jonesing for some French onion," she said with a shrug. "I suppose it's too much to expect that you read my mind."

"Uh, yeah," Rooster said, setting the groceries on the counter. "I'll leave that to the professionals."

"Funny," Josie said, gently punching him on the shoulder.

"So, what's the surprise?" I said, glancing around the kitchen.

"It's in the living room," Rooster said. "Head on in. I'll be there as soon as I put the groceries away."

We walked into the living room and immediately felt the heat from the roaring fire. Lacey was stretched out on a couch reading a book. Lying on the couch with its head nestled against her shoulder was the Utonagan. When she heard us, Lacey put her book down and sat up. The dog hopped off the couch and greeted us.

"Okay," I said with a grin. "I'm officially surprised."

"Hi, guys," Lacey said. "We were too. Last night, we heard this scratching on the front door, and when we opened it, Akna trotted in like she owned the place. She said hello then stretched out in front of the fire. And apart from going out to take care of business, she hasn't gotten more than ten feet away from either one of us."

"She must have been a house dog," I said, stroking the Utonagan's head. "Before Peters got...sorry, Lacey."

"Don't worry about it," Lacey said through a sad smile.

Rooster entered and stoked the fire before adding a fresh log. He sat down next to Lacey and petted the dog who was already laying at his feet.

"You've made a new friend," Josie said.

"Yeah, she's a good dog," Rooster said.

"Is she showing any strange behavior?" Josie said.

"You mean wolf-like?" he said.

"Yeah."

"Not a trace," Rooster said. "But don't worry, I'm keeping a close eye on her."

"Have you found any records around the place?" I said.

"Of Jeremy's work with the hybrids?" Lacey said. "Not a thing. I was hoping there might be something on his computer."

"No, there's not," I said. "And believe me, I've been looking."

Josie snorted.

"Shut it," I said, giving her the evil eye. "He must have everything written down somewhere. Nobody would spend that much time manipulating their genes and not keep track of it."

"No, they wouldn't," Lacey said. "Especially Jeremy."

"What's the update on the investigation?" Rooster said.

"That's right," I said. "We haven't had a chance to talk."

"So, you do have some news," he said, giving the dog a final pet before giving me his undivided attention.

"I do."

I spent a few minutes reviewing the past few days in detail. As I talked, both Rooster and Lacey listened closely and occasionally shared baffled looks with each other. When I finished, I got up and stood with my back to the fire. I gently rubbed my stomach as I waited for questions.

"He wrote himself in as a beneficiary?" Rooster said. "What the hell was he thinking?"

"That he could get away with it would be my first guess," I said with a shrug.

"If Jeremy was dead, it's not that hard to believe," Lacey said.

"But she said Lamplighter's assistant signed as a witness," Rooster said. "If the two versions of the will are different, that person would certainly recognize it."

"I knew I forgot to mention something," I said. "The witness is dead."

"Althea's dead?" Rooster said, stunned.

"She is," I said. "You knew her?"

"I did," he said. "Geez, that sucks. She was a nice kid. A little troubled, but a good person. What happened to her?"

"Her car went off a mountain road in Colorado," I said.

"How convenient for Larry," Rooster said. "The cops are seriously looking at him, right?"

"They are," I said, nodding. "But something doesn't seem right about it."

"I have no trouble making it work," Josie said. "The guy writes himself into the will, then takes Larry out. After that, the only loose end would be the witness. And, miracles of miracles, her car goes off a cliff."

"I know," I said, frowning. "But still."

"Well, far be it for me to question your snooping abilities, but sometimes things are exactly the way they appear."

"You're probably right," I said. "But I can't get the look on Larry's face out of my mind when he heard Peters was dead. I grew up with the guy, and he was never known for his poker face."

"He's a lawyer," Josie said. "He probably developed it over the years. Along with a host of other wonderful traits. Like staging slip and sue accidents."

"That's a long way from killing two people," I said.

"The degree of the crime is often directly proportional to the amount of money involved," Rooster said.

"Who said that?" Josie said, glancing at him.

"I did."

"Funny."

"I think I'll make a pot of coffee," Lacey said, getting to her feet.

"Sounds great," Josie said.

"No, thanks, Lacey," I said. "I've had my daily limit."

"Hot chocolate?"

"Oh, perfect. Thanks."

"How about you, Rooster?" Lacey said.

"Coffee would be great. Thanks."

"With a little splash of brandy," she said, grinning at him. "Just the way you like it."

She headed off to the kitchen trailed by the Utonagan. Josie gave Rooster a goofy grin then flashed me a conspiratorially sideways glance.

"I think Rooster's got himself a girlfriend," Josie said.

"Yes, I noticed," I said, laughing.

"Don't start," he said, going for indignation but coming up short.

"Oh, it's too late for that," Josie said, glancing around the room. "Yeah, it's nice and cozy. Tucked way out in the woods."

"With a full wine cellar," I chimed in. "Crackling fire. No chance of anybody popping in to interrupt the flow."

"Interrupt the flow?" Rooster said, frowning at me. "You are so weird."

"She is," Josie said, laughing. "But you're...*in love*."

"What are you, twelve?" he said.

"I think we touched a nerve," Josie said to me.

"Josie, has anybody told you what a total pain in the butt you can be?" Rooster said.

"Not today."

Rooster shook his head then continued.

"She's a very nice woman," he said. "And we get along great. What's wrong with that?"

"Are you going to mention the age difference, or should I?" Josie said to me.

"Age is just a number," Rooster said, then focused on me. "And I used your mother's formula. We're fine."

"Her formula?" Josie said, staring at me, confused by his comment.

"Half your age plus seven," I said with a shrug. "She calls it the outer-band of the age range for dating somebody."

Josie gave it some thought and was apparently running some of the math in her head.

"Hey, that's not bad," she said.

"Well, I'm happy for you guys. I hope it works out."

"It's way too early to worry about that," Rooster said. "But I do have to say I'm enjoying our time out here."

153

"You're convinced she's not involved in any of this," I said.

"I'm positive," Rooster said.

"Okay," I said softly. "But if somehow turns out she is, what then?"

"I'd be crushed."

Chapter 15

The restaurant parking lot was fuller than we had expected. We entered through the kitchen and found Chef Claire busily working her way through a long line of orders attached at eye level. She glanced up briefly when she heard us come in, gave us a small wave then barked at Charlie, her sous chef.

"I'm still waiting for a side of spaghetti."

"We're a minute away," Charlie said, doing his best octopus imitation as he worked on several plates.

"What the heck is going on?" I said.

"There's some sort of spring boat show going on," Chef Claire said.

"Yeah, but that's over in Kingston," I said, surprised.

"Well, apparently, a bunch of them decided to caravan over here for dinner," she said, motioning for us to get out of the kitchen.

"Nice to see you get right back into mid-season form," Josie said, laughing as she headed for the door that led to the dining room. "I thought you'd need at least a couple of weeks of spring training."

Chef Claire fired a dinner roll that hit Josie in the back of the head.

"Nice shot," I said.

Josie bent down to retrieve the roll then took a bite.

"Thanks, Chef Claire," she said, chewing. "Not as good as the rustic Italian, but not bad."

"Unbelievable," I said, then gently shoved her through the door. "I can't believe you ate that after it was on the floor."

"That's why they give us an immune system," she said, heading straight for the lounge. "And that kitchen floor is immaculate."

"We must have a different definition," I said, easing my way into one of the stools at the bar. "Hey, Millie."

"Hi, guys," she said, barely looking up. "I'll be with you in a sec. I'm dealing with a landslide of orders at the moment."

"Take your time," I said, glancing around the crowded lounge and waving to several people I knew. Then my eyes landed on two people sitting on a couch near the fireplace. "Huh? What do you know?"

"What is it?" Josie said, scanning the room.

"By the fire," I said, nodding in the general direction. "Larry the Loser."

"Is that Marjorie Young with him?"

"It is," I said, frowning. "That's odd."

"It has to be business-related, right?"

"Let's hope so," I said, shaking my head. "She's way out of his league."

"Maybe she has legal problems."

"And she called him?"

Larry got up from the couch and headed for the bar carrying two empty glasses. When he spotted me, he made a beeline for us and came to a stop between our stools. He smiled at both of us, lingered on Josie a bit too long then set the glasses down on the bar.

"How are you doing tonight?"

"We're great, Larry," I said. "Are you here for dinner or just drinks?"

"Dinner," he said. "Assuming a table ever opens up. I didn't expect it to be this crowded."

"Is that Marjorie?" I said.

"It is," he said, glancing over at her. "You remember that opportunity I mentioned?"

"I do."

"Well, she's it."

"Really?" I said, surprised. "You're going to be managing her portfolio?"

"Only a bit of it for now," Larry said. "Marjorie said she always starts off new financial managers with just a taste. You know, to see how well they do."

"Then she must have a lot of financial managers," I said, laughing.

"Yeah, she is loaded, isn't she?" Larry said with a grin. "Probably right up with your mom."

"If the rumors are to be believed, I'm sure she is," I said, waving to her. "I haven't seen her in a while. I think I'll go say hi."

I ignored the dirty look Josie was giving me for leaving her alone with the lawyer and made my way through the crowd to where the woman was sitting.

"Hello, Marjorie," I said, beaming at her.

"Suzy," she said, patting the couch next to her. "Look at you. Please, sit down and get off your feet."

"As long as you promise to help me back up," I said, easing my way onto the thick cushion. "How are you?"

"I'm doing very well, thank you," she said, draping an arm over the couch and doing a half-turn toward me. "You're positively glowing."

"Thanks," I said. "People are always saying that. But I don't get it. It must be one of those social conventions."

"It's probably better than saying you're bigger than a house, right?" she said with a grin.

I laughed and patted my stomach.

"How's your mom?"

"She's a force of nature."

"She is indeed. Please send her my best," Marjorie said.

"I'll do that," I said, then tossed my line into the water. "I see you're here with Larry."

"I am," she said, nodding. "Against the advice of my family, I've decided to give him a chance to see if he can make me some money."

"I see. So, you do know his reputation?"

"I do," she said. "But he's adamant his days of staging accidents are over."

"I'm sure he believes that," I whispered.

"What's that?"

"Nothing," I said. "It's none of my business, but he seems like an odd choice."

"There's no doubt about it. He is. But his father was good friends with my late husband, may he rest in peace. And Larry recently called me out of the blue. He said he had just gotten certified as a financial planner, and I was his first call."

"And you decided to hire him?"

"I did," she said, her eyes twinkling with mischief. "I like to keep all my money managers on their toes. And believe me, when they heard I was hiring Larry, I got their attention in a hurry."

"Probably not a bad strategy," I said, nodding.

"It might be something for you to consider," she said. "Because at some point, you'll have the same problem I do."

"When you no longer have to worry about making money, the problem becomes hanging onto it," I said, reciting my mother's mantra.

"You've learned well, my dear," she said, patting my hand. "But don't worry, I'm sure your mother is several steps ahead of that problem."

"Are you sure Larry is up to it?"

"Rule number one. Make the amount big enough to get the person's attention, but not enough to hurt you if things go south," she said. "And Larry's hungry. I like all my financial advisors hungry. And competing with each other."

"You're giving him a chance to make a fresh start," I said. "That's very nice of you, Marjorie."

"Nice doesn't have anything to do with it. Let's call it a favor with some clearly defined benchmarks attached to it."

"Well, I hope he doesn't screw it up," I said.

"Me too," she said. "For both our sakes."

"I should get back," I said, gently rocking back and forth on the couch to build up some momentum. "Josie gets cranky when she hasn't eaten."

"She truly is a remarkable looking woman," Marjorie said, studying Josie who was giving Larry her best bobblehead nod as he prattled on about something. "How is it possible she's still unattached?"

"She sets an impossibly high standard for herself," I said, getting to my feet. "And that carries over into what she expects from her relationships. Some people might call it a character flaw."

"I'd call it a personal strength," Marjorie said firmly. "Never settle for close enough."

"Good advice. Make sure you share that one with Larry."

"Don't worry. I already have," she said, extending her hand. "You take good care of yourself, Suzy."

"You too, Marjorie," I said, then headed back to the bar, thoroughly confused with my neurons on fire.

Chapter 16

The reading of Dr. Jeremy Peters' will occurred on a Thursday in the midst of a cold, driving rainstorm that was rapidly removing the remnants of our winter snow. From the warmth of the van we used to transport dogs, I turned the wipers off then did the same with the engine. We were parked on a dead-end street near Larry the Loser's house safely out of sight. I glanced over at the Chief who was in the passenger seat then through the rear-view mirror at Detective Williams.

"You guys okay with the engine off or do you need the heater?"

"I'm fine," Detective Williams said. "Are you sure we're going to be able to hear them?"

I grabbed the laser microphone from a duffel bag and showed it to the detective. Then I attached it to the side mirror.

"It'll be like we're in the room with them," I said. "This thing is amazing. It works off vibrations and somehow is capable of going through windows."

"You don't say," Detective Williams said.

"That's right," I said, mildly embarrassed. "You guys must use these things all the time."

"You and your toys," Detective Williams said, shaking his head.

"Hey, some people collect stamps. I like hi-tech gadgets," I said, switching the microphone on. I handed them both earpieces then inserted my own. "Hey, look at that."

"What?" the Chief said, following my eyes.

"Right over there," I said, pointing. "An actual patch of grass. We'll be out on the River before we know it."

"If it keeps raining like this, the street will be a river," the Chief said, then spotted a car coming to a stop directly in front of Larry's office. "Here we go."

I picked up my binoculars and scanned the two people who were doing their best to get under the umbrella they were sharing.

"She must be Peters' wife," I said, handing the binoculars to the Chief. "I don't have a clue who the guy is."

"He must be the brother," Detective Williams said.

"Probably," the Chief said, studying them through the glasses. "It's hard to tell, but I think I see a resemblance."

"Where does he live?" I said.

"Vegas," Detective Williams said. "He works at one of the casinos. Blackjack dealer."

"What about the wife?" I said. "Where does she live?"

"New York," Detective Williams said. "She's an art history professor. And she's also a consultant to some of the galleries in the City."

We watched as they headed inside. Moments later, Lacey's SUV came to a stop in front of the house. Lacey hopped out and pulled the hood of her rain slicker up as she raced to the front steps. When she reached the porch, she lowered the hood. I glanced over at the Chief who had the binoculars on her.

"How does she look?" I said.

"Nervous."

"She probably can't wait to hear what Peters left her," Detective Williams said.

"Or she's nervous about being in the same room with the wife," I said as I watched Lacey head inside.

We sat in silence for another few minutes until a sleek Mercedes came to a stop behind Lacey's vehicle.

"Nice car," the Chief said.

"That's the S65," I said. "My mom has been talking about getting one."

"What the heck is she going to do with another car?" the Chief said.

"Rhetorical, right?"

"She keeps it up, she's going to have to build a new garage," the Chief said. "But it sure is a nice set of wheels. How much do they go for?"

"More than your house," I said, spotting another car arriving. "That looks like a rental."

"It does," Detective Williams said. "It must be Clarissa George."

I watched as the woman climbed out of her car and raced for the house. The driver of the Mercedes also got out and jogged down the sidewalk. He bounded up the steps and extended his hand to the woman named Clarissa. I glanced over at the Chief who had the binoculars on them.

"Did that look like a handshake between two people who'd never met?" I said.

"It did," Chief Abrams said, nodding. He glanced over his shoulder into the backseat. "What did you find out about those two?"

"At one point, the woman was Peters' assistant. Or still is. Or was until…" Detective Williams said. "Well, you know."

"Got it."

"The guy is Charles Howard. A bit of a mystery man. He's an entrepreneur. You know, investor type who dabbles in startups."

"What sort of companies does he invest in?" I said.

"Tech. Biomed. Stuff like that," Detective Williams said.

"Why the heck would he be interested in Peters' work with wolves?" I said.

"Who knows?" Detective Williams said with a shrug. "That's all of them, right?"

"It is," I said, adjusting the volume on the microphone.

"I can't wait to hear how Larry plays this," Detective Williams said with a laugh.

"He didn't do it," I said, staring at the detective through the rear-view mirror.

"Don't start," the Chief said, glancing back and forth at both of us. "I can't listen to you two debate it again."

"What do you want to bet?" Detective Williams said.

"A bag of bite-sized."

"You're on," he said. "There's no way the lawyer didn't do it."

"We'll see."

Then we heard Larry the Loser's voice clear as day through our earpieces.

"I'd like to thank all of you for coming in on such a crappy day," the lawyer said. "And I'd like to extend my sincere condolences for your loss. Jeremy was a truly unique individual, and we're all worse off with his tragic passing."

"Unique?" a woman's voice said.

"That's how I would describe him, Mrs. Peters," Larry said softly.

"Call me Charlotte. My days of being called Mrs. Peters are officially over."

"Harsh," I whispered.

"Yeah," the Chief said. "So much for mourning her dead husband."

"I'm sorry," Lacey said. "But could we do introductions?"

"Of course," Larry said. "I'm so sorry. I assumed you all knew each other." We heard him clear his throat. "This is Charlotte Peters. Jeremy's wife. To her right is Lacey Adams."

"The trollop he was with before he dumped you to start up with that one," Charlotte said.

"Trollop?" Lacey said, her voice rising.

"You heard me," Charlotte said. "Trollop one, meet trollop number two."

"There's no need for that, Charlotte," a man said. "I'm Peter. Jeremy's brother."

"Peter Peters?" I said, surprised. "As in pumpkin eater?"

"Man, his parents were cruel," the Chief said.

"It's nice to meet you, Peter," Lacey said. "Jeremy always spoke fondly of you."

"Not a chance," Peter said with a laugh. "And call me P-Squared."

"P-Squared?" Lacey said.

"It's what all my friends call me," he said. "You know, a play on my double name."

"Okay," Lacey said, obviously confused. "I'm Lacey."

"It's nice to meet you. I'm Clarissa George. Jeremy's research assistant."

"So, you're the one," the brother said.

"She is indeed," Charlotte said with a laugh. "What do you think, *P-Squared*? Is trollop two an upgrade over version one, or not?"

"Charlotte, please," the brother said. "Hi, I'm Jeremy's brother, Peter."

"Yes, I heard. I've been following along. I'm Charles Howard. It's nice to meet you. All of you."

"How did you know my brother?"

"I was one of his investors."

"You invested in his wolf research?" Lacey said.

"Of course," Charles Howard said.

"He's lying," I whispered.

"He certainly is," Detective Williams said.

"Charles, it's been a long time. And I must say it is nice seeing you," Charlotte said. "But I must ask. What on earth could Jeremy possibly have left you in his will?"

"I don't have a clue, Charlotte," Charles said. "The lawyer called my office and said I should be here for the reading. So, here I am. And I'm on a tight schedule. Can we get on with it?"

"Of course," Larry said, then cleared his throat again. "I'm sorry I didn't get a chance to mail you a copy of the will before today. But things happened so fast, I thought I'd just wait. Let me pass these out."

We heard the sound of papers being shuffled, and a long silence ensued.

"What you have in front of you is the will itself," Larry said eventually. "It outlines Jeremy's general intentions and lists the beneficiaries. All the beneficiaries are listed on page one. The document referenced on page two, known as Schedule A, details how Jeremy's assets are to be distributed. That document, the sole copy, has been sealed and locked in my safe since the day it was drawn up. As soon as you're ready, I will read it to you, per Jeremy's instructions."

"When was this drawn up?" Charlotte said.

"The date is on the last page next to the signatures," Larry said.

"What are you trying to pull here?" Charlotte said.

"I'm sorry," Larry said. "I'm not sure I understand your question."

"Then let me be perfectly clear," Charlotte said. "How was it possible for you to draft the will?"

"It was really quite simple," Larry said, confused. "I use a standard template. All we needed to do was enter the information as dictated by Jeremy."

"That's not what I'm talking about. Are you really this dumb or just acting to throw us off the scent?"

"Mrs. Peters…uh, Charlotte," Larry said, on the defensive. "I really don't have a clue what you're talking about."

"How could you draft the will while also being listed as one of the beneficiaries?"

"What?" Larry whispered.

"Isn't that your name on the top of page two?" Charlotte said.

A lengthy silence ensued, followed by Larry's nervous cough.

"How is this possible?" Larry said. "I swear. I had no idea I was listed as a beneficiary."

"But you drew up the document, right?" P-Squared said.

"I did. But there was never a mention of me being one of the beneficiaries. I swear on my mother's grave."

"Beautiful," Charles Howard said, obviously bemused by what he was hearing.

"If Larry's lying, he's really good at it," I said.

"Even for a lawyer," Chief Abrams said.

"Shhh," Detective Williams said, leaning forward and listening closely to the conversation.

"This is weird," Clarissa said. "How could you not know you were one of the beneficiaries?"

"But I'm not one of the beneficiaries," Larry said, his voice quivering like a young kid caught in the act.

"Did you hear that?" the Chief said.

"What?" I said, cocking my head.

"That was the sound of Larry's legal career being flushed down the toilet."

"I told you he didn't do it," I said, glancing into the backseat.

"Not so fast," Detective Williams said. "Let's see how it plays out."

"Now what?" P-Squared said.

"I guess we should hear how Jeremy wanted his assets distributed," Charles Howard said.

"This oughta be good," Charlotte said, the contempt in her voice unmistakable.

We heard the sound of a chair being pushed back from the table and the murmur of whispered table talk. Moments later, we heard someone sit back down.

"This is the envelope containing Schedule A," Jeremy said. "As you can see, the seal is unbroken."

"Like that would have been a problem to pull off," Charlotte said. "Go ahead, read it."

We heard the sound of an envelope being opened and, once again, Larry cleared his throat before speaking.

"Item one. To my wife, Charlotte, I leave our home in New York and all personal belongings contained therein."

"You live in the City?" Clarissa said.

"Yeah," Charlotte said. "It's a three-story brownstone in Brooklyn."

"Nice," Clarissa said.

"Two mortgages and a property tax bill that could choke a horse," Charlotte snapped. "Yeah, real nice. What else did he leave me?"

"Uh…nothing," Larry said.

"Unbelievable," she said.

"Should I continue?"

"Why stop now?" Charlotte said.

"Item two. To my brother, Peter, an inveterate gambler who continues to go through life with no sense of purpose or direction, I leave the sum of one thousand dollars. It is my sincere hope he uses the money on some meaningless game of chance. I also hope he loses it immediately. May it serve as a reminder to him of a life thrown away."

"A thousand bucks?" P-Squared said. "I came all this way to hear that? Thanks a lot, brother."

"You think you got problems?" Charlotte said. "Try paying my mortgage for a month. Get on with this charade."

"Item three. To my current research assistant, Clarissa George, I leave my signed, first-edition copy of Charles Darwin's, On the Origin of Species."

"Wow," Clarissa said.

"He left you a book?" P-Squared said, laughing. "Now, I don't feel so bad."

"You idiot," Charlotte said. "That book has to be worth a hundred grand."

"What?" P-Squared said. "What it's printed on? Hundreds?"

"I don't believe it," Clarissa said.

"Too bad she's never going to get her hands on it," I said.

"Yeah, the wife's lawyer is going to have a field day with this," Detective Williams said.

"Item four," Larry said, after clearing his throat again. "To my former assistant, Lacey Adams, I leave all my research into wolf-hybrids. She's the only person who ever fully understood what I was trying to achieve, and I hope with all my heart that she will continue to pursue my research goals. To that end, I also leave her Cabot Lodge to use as a home for my beloved hybrids where she can carry out her work. The annual operating costs of the research, along with the costs required to maintain Cabot Lodge, are to be paid from my general operating account."

"What?" Lacey said.

"You heard the man," Charlotte snapped. "You get to play with the animals. Whatever the heck they are."

"But I never said I understood or appreciated what he was trying to do," Lacey said, protesting. "In fact, I always hated what he was doing."

"I'm sorry to interrupt," Charles Howard. "But what the heck is Cabot Lodge?"

"It's some old hunting lodge Jeremy inherited from his old man," Charlotte said. "I think it's around here somewhere. Apparently, the place is in ruins."

"Actually, it's not," Lacey said. "It's very nice."

"Interesting. I assume you two used to use it as a love nest?" Charlotte said.

"We did not," Lacey snapped. "In fact, I'd never been there until a few days ago."

"What were you doing there?" Charlotte said.

"Trying to track down one of Jeremy's dogs. I'm staying there at the moment."

"Doing what?" Charlotte said.

"Looking after his hybrids, what else?"

"Well, don't get used to it," Charlotte said. "As soon as I get a handle on what this shyster is trying to pull, you'll be out of there. And all those horrid creatures will be put down."

"Put down? Over my dead body," Lacey said.

"Good girl," I said, nodding.

"Can we please get this over with?" Charles Howard said.

"We're almost done," Larry said. "There's just one more item to go." He cleared his throat again then continued. "Item five. This deals with the management and disbursement of funds from Jeremy's general operating account."

"Did you get a chance to look into that account yet?" I said to Detective Williams.

"We did. There's almost eight million in it."

"Geez," I grunted.

"Okay, if I could have your attention, I'll read the final item," Larry said. "Oh, my word. What the heck?"

"What is it now?" Charlotte said.

"There must be some sort of mistake," Larry said. "This item was supposed to have your name next to it."

"Mine?" Charles Howard said. "Was?"

"Yes," Larry said, apparently gulping down a large drink of water. "Item five. To my new friend and attorney, Lawrence Lamplighter, I leave full control of the management and disbursement of funds from my general operating account. Unless otherwise outlined in this, my last will and testament, Mr. Lamplighter has sole discretion regarding how funds from this account shall be used."

"Are you freaking kidding me?" Charlotte said. "Did you really think you were going to get away with this?"

"I'm as surprised as you are, Charlotte. You have to believe me. I had no idea about any of this."

"It doesn't matter," Charlotte said. "This will isn't worth the paper it's written on. And you, my shyster friend, have spent your last days as a lawyer."

"But he's just starting his days as a felon," I whispered.

"I thought you were convinced he didn't do it," Detective Williams said.

"I am," I said through the rear-view mirror. "But how the heck is Larry going to beat the murder charge? Houdini couldn't get out of this one."

"Can't argue with that," Chief Abrams said. "Man, whoever is setting Larry up sure did a good job. This thing looks airtight."

"I don't believe it," Larry said. "Jeremy specifically named Charles as the trustee of those funds."

"Him?" Charlotte said. "Why him?"

"I assume because it's pretty much my money," Charles said.

"How much money are we talking about?" Charlotte said.

"I have no idea," Larry said. "Jeremy wouldn't talk about it."

"Do you know?" Charlotte said.

"No, I don't have a clue," Charles said. "But unless Jeremy went on a recent spending spree, it's somewhere in the millions."

"This isn't going to stand," Charlotte said. "I'm going to call my lawyer. And you're gonna wish you'd decided to become a garbage collector by the time this is over."

"This isn't possible," Larry said.

"It should be easy enough to check," Charles said.

"How's that?" Charlotte said.

"We just need to talk to the person who witnessed the signing," he said.

"Althea," Larry whispered.

"I assume you have her phone number," Charles said.

"She recently left the area," Larry said. "And I haven't been able to get in touch with her."

"I'm sure the police will be able to track her down," Charlotte said, then exhaled loudly. "Okay, here's what we're going to do. I'm going to call my lawyer. Then we're going to sit down later today and discuss what he recommends. Is there another place we could meet? Somewhere other than this rathole."

"Hey," Larry said, protesting. "What's wrong with my office?"

"I'm surprised you even have to ask," Charlotte said.

"C's," Lacey said softly. "It's a local restaurant."

"Perfect," I whispered.

"Yeah, that was well done," the Chief said.

"That should work," Charlotte said. "Seven o'clock. By then, I should have a better idea about who I'm going to sue. Or send to jail."

"What now?" I said to Detective Williams.

"Well, we go to dinner tonight," he said. "And at some point in the evening, I'll swing by their table and let them know I'd like all of them to stick around for a few days."

"Any idea who it might be?" I said.

"Right now, I'm leaning toward the wife," he said.

"Yeah, me too," the Chief said.

I frowned and gave it some thought.

"It seems too easy," I said, then glanced in the rear-view mirror. "You convinced now that Larry didn't do it?"

"Don't gloat," Detective Williams said with a laugh. "You do know that you're a really bad winner."

"One bag of bite-sized, please. And no skimping. I want the party pack."

Chapter 17

I sat quietly, staring into the fire, my neurons relentless. I toyed with what was left of my dessert then set my fork down and pushed my plate away.

"Dollar for your thoughts?" Josie said.

"A whole dollar?"

"You seem to have a lot on your mind," she said with a grin. "Offering a penny would be lowballing you."

"Well, I should warn you. You get what you pay for. Right now, my thoughts are a mess."

"I know I'm going to regret this," she said. "But do you want to talk about it?"

"I guess my first question is why would anybody want to kill Peters over a bunch of wolf hybrids?"

"I think we both know the answer to that one. Nobody would."

"Yeah," I said, sitting back on the couch and rubbing my stomach. "Then the motive has to be jealousy or money. Maybe both."

"The wife?" Josie said, then took a sip of Limoncello.

"That's what the Chief and Detective Williams think. As soon as Peters will is declared null and void, which it will be, they're convinced she's going to get everything."

"It sounds pretty straightforward," Josie said. "The scorned wife seeking revenge and wanting to get her hands on his money."

"I suppose," I said, rubbing my forehead. "Althea is the key to this thing."

"But she's dead."

"It's always something, right?"

"There's that sense of humor," Josie said. "Larry the Loser seemed genuinely surprised today?"

"He did. And there was no way he was going to get away with it," I said. "Unless he was playing dumb when he read the thing and tries to tough out whatever threats or lawsuit the wife throws at him. But he was clearly shocked by what was in that version of the will. And he made no effort to hide it."

"If the wife was behind it, how the heck did she cross paths with Althea?"

"That, my friend, is a very good question."

"Do you think Larry is going to be charged with Peters' murder?"

"I don't think the cops have any other option," I said, again rubbing my forehead.

"Even though the Chief and Detective Williams don't think he did it?" Josie said, frowning.

"He was caught red-handed writing himself in as a beneficiary then listing himself as the sole trustee of a multi-million-dollar account. And the only person who might be able to clear him went off a cliff. I think the cops and lawyers call that a smoking gun."

"Then I guess you'll have to figure out what's going on, right?"

"That's the plan."

"So, you've got one?"

"Right now, all I've got is a jigsaw puzzle with a bunch of missing pieces."

"You'll figure it out."

"I need to talk to Larry."

"Well, here's your chance," Josie said, nodding at the end of the bar where Larry was sitting by himself slumped over his drink. "But you better hurry. It looks he's been here awhile."

"Why not?" I said, slowly working my way off the couch onto my feet. "Wish me luck."

I headed for the bar and gently tapped the lawyer on the shoulder. He did a half-turn and forced a smile.

"Hey, Suzy. Have a seat."

"No, I think I better stay upright. I almost didn't make it off the couch."

"It's quite a load you're carrying. I'll give you that," he said, giving me a quick once-over.

"Load?"

"Sorry. Bad choice of words."

"Don't worry about it. I heard you had the reading of Jeremy Peters' will today," I said, going for casual.

"Where did you hear that?" he said, raising an eyebrow at me.

"Small town," I said, rocking back and forth on my heels. "So, can I assume everyone was happy with the news?"

Larry snorted then drained the last of his drink. I caught Millie's eye and motioned for another round.

"Let's say I've had better days and leave it at that," he said, crunching an ice cube.

"Where's the fun in that, Larry?" I said, gently punching him on the shoulder.

He stared at me as if I had somehow invaded his personal space then shrugged.

"I think I'm being set up," he said, taking a sip of his fresh drink.

"For what?" I said, deciding to play my cards close.

"Peters' murder. What else?"

"Who would want to do that to you?"

"Althea is my best guess at the moment," he said, draining half his drink. "I definitely need to have a little chat with her, but she's nowhere to be found."

"This is none of my business, but what sort of relationship did the two of you have?"

"At first, it was great," he whispered. "Then it went south in a hurry."

"What happened?"

"I really don't know. One day, we're talking about moving in together, the next she's making plans to move to Colorado. Without me."

"I'm sorry to hear that," I said. "Why don't you tell me what happened today?"

To my surprise, he did. I listened closely to his description of the reading, a very accurate overview of what we'd heard. When he finished, he stared at me again, obviously waiting for a response.

"Well?" he said, after a long pause.

"I have to agree with you, Larry. It sounds like somebody is setting you up."

"But why would Althea do it?"

"What was her involvement with Peters' will?" I said, tossing my line in the water.

"She pretty much handled all of it," he said. "And she also signed off as the witness."

"The three of you signed the will in your office?"

"Nah, I left that to her," he said, swirling the ice in his glass. "I signed it later after it was written up."

"But you met with Peters, didn't you?"

"Only briefly. Althea brought him to me as a client. We chatted for a few minutes, then I left the office to study."

"Study?" I said, confused.

"For my Series 6 exam."

"Series 6?"

"Yeah, it's the test you have to pass to be licensed to sell financial products. You know, mutual funds, annuities, stuff like that."

"Sure, sure."

"That test is a mother, so I was studying like crazy for months. During that time, Althea pretty much ran my practice. I'd show up for certain meetings and sign off on various documents."

"But you read the will, right?"

"I scanned it," he said with a shrug. "It was pretty standard, and Althea walked me through the main points."

"Geez, Larry," I said, frowning at him. "You didn't even read the thing?"

"Like I said, I was busy. And I trusted her completely."

"Got it," I whispered. "Do you remember anything Althea told you?"

"I remember Peters' left the house to his wife. And the guy who was supposed to get control of the money. I vaguely remember some of the names of the other beneficiaries. That's about it."

"Why do you think Althea listed you as a beneficiary and the trustee of Peters' money?"

"Obviously it was part of whatever setup this is," he said, waving his empty glass at Millie.

"Please, don't do that," I said, scowling at him.

"Do what?"

"Wave your glass at Millie like that," I said. "She's a server, not your *servant*."

"I'm sorry," he said, giving me a confused stare. "Geez, what brought that on?"

186

"The people who work here are family," I said, still agitated. "And family members are to be treated with respect." Then my neurons flared and I flinched.

"Are you okay?" Larry said. "Is the baby kicking?"

"No, I'm fine," I said, taking a few deep breaths. "Who else was at the reading today?"

"Your new vet was there. Peters left her his wolf research, whatever the heck that is. And he also gave her some hunting lodge out in the woods."

"Yeah, she mentioned it."

"Not that she's going to get her hands on it after the wife gets through with me. He gave a rare book to one of his research assistants. And his brother got a thousand bucks. Man, he was not a happy guy."

"No, he wasn't," I said, deep in thought.

"What?"

"I said I'm sure he wasn't," I said, recovering quickly. "Was anybody else there?"

"Just the guy who was supposed to get control of Peters' funds. Charles Howard."

"How did he take the news?"

"Nothing seemed to faze the guy," Larry said. "He made a few comments, even laughed a couple of times after it became clear things were heading south in a hurry. But he barely blinked when the wife started talking about getting the will invalidated. If I was about to be cut out of a deal like that, I doubt if I'd be that calm."

"Maybe he had something bigger in mind," I said, unsure where the comment came from.

"Like what?"

"I don't have a clue," I said, shrugging.

"He's a money guy," Larry said. "And one of Peters' major investors. But how could there be any money in wolf research?"

"That's a very good question, Larry."

"Thanks. I occasionally ask them," he said, taking another long sip from his drink.

"How many of those have you had?" I said, nodding at his glass.

"More than one."

"You might want to keep a clear head."

"I'll worry about that tomorrow," he said, draining his glass. He was about to wave it in the air when he stopped and waited patiently until he caught Millie's eye. He grinned at me. "Better?"

"Much," I said, laughing.

"I just can't figure out why Althea would do that to me."

"Love or money," I said without hesitation. "Or love *of* money."

"You think she's getting a cut?"

"Not anymore," I whispered, deciding the news about the woman's death should come from the cops and not from me.

"Yeah, I imagine whatever scam she was working has probably crashed and burned."

"I'm sure you're right," I said, frowning at the thought of Althea's car going off the mountain. "Okay, Larry. I need to get going. It's been a long day."

"You'll get no argument from me," he said, sipping his fresh drink. "But tomorrow has to be better, right?"

"As long as you don't try to drive yourself home tonight, I'm sure it will be." I caught Millie's eye and motioned her over. "Keys, Larry."

"What?"

"Give Millie your car keys," I said. "You can pick them up tomorrow."

"You're taking my keys?"

"We are," I said. "Somebody will give you a lift home."

"Nah, that's fine," he said, handing Millie his keys. "I'll just walk."

"Good idea. The fresh air will do you good."

"Okay," he said, draining his glass. "If I'm walking, then I'm gonna keep drinking."

Chapter 18

I shuffled back and forth on my feet in front of the fire, my movements severely limited due to my condition. But despite my lack of physical progress, my mind was going a thousand miles an hour. Rooster watched me with a puzzled look and eventually had to ask.

"What on earth are you doing?"

"She's pacing," Josie said as she eyed the appetizer tray on the coffee table in front of her.

"Thanks for clarifying," Rooster said.

"She's right," I said, coming to a stop. "It's the best I can do these days."

"I would have gone with marching in place, but that's just me," Rooster said.

Lacey entered the room carrying a pot of coffee and four mugs. She set them down on the coffee table, sampled from the tray, then poured.

"How are the hybrids doing?" I said.

"As well as can be expected," Lacey said. "It's not much of a life being caged up like that."

"How's the litter of pups?" Josie said.

"They're gorgeous," Lacey said. "I think they're about a week away from being ready for some solid food."

"How much wolf do you think they have in them?" I said, resuming my pacing.

"More than I care to think about," Lacey said. "What are the cops saying?"

"Well, the good news is you're pretty much off the hook," I said.

"Even though Jeremy left me this place?"

"Nobody knows for sure what he left to anybody," I said. "But you're way down the list of suspects."

"And Larry?" Rooster said.

"That's where it starts to get weird," I said. "The Chief and Detective Williams are almost positive he didn't do it. But he's probably still going to be charged with Peters' murder."

"Almost positive?" Rooster said, raising an eyebrow. "They're hedging their bets?"

"I don't know if I'd call it hedging. It's more like they're just baffled," I said, then took a sip of coffee.

"I feel bad about spending so much time out here," Lacey said. "I just start working for you guys, and I end up being AWOL most of the time."

"Don't worry about it," Josie said. "I'm happy to cover it until things clear up."

"Thanks, Josie. What are we going to do with them?"

"I have no idea," I said. "But one thing we're definitely going to do is make sure Peters' wife never gets her hands on them."

"She was pretty clear about wanting to put them down," Lacey said.

"As were you when you told her over your dead body," I said. "How did she react when you said that?"

"She gave me her best death stare," Lacey said. "But I think she was worried about other things."

"Like getting her hands on her dead husband's money," Josie said, reaching for a bacon-wrapped jalapeno popper. She nodded her approval as she worked her way through it. "These are excellent, Rooster."

"Thanks," he said, reaching for one. "Chef Claire gave me the recipe. The secret is to grill the jalapenos first."

"I wish other secrets were a bit easier to uncover," I said, resuming my pacing again as I glanced around the enormous room. "If you do somehow end up owning this place, those stuffed animal heads really need to go."

"Tell me about it," Lacey said with a laugh.

"But I do like that wolf painting," I said, focusing on the large canvas hanging on one of the walls.

"Yeah, me too," Rooster said, studying the painting of a solitary wolf baying while bathed in moonlight. "It really captures the spirit and determination of the lone wolf."

"Well, look at you," Josie said. "Well done, Art."

"Art?" Rooster said, frowning at her.

"Yeah. Art Critic. Jack London would be so proud."

"And you call her weird," Rooster said to Josie as he nodded in my direction.

"Jeremy used to have that painting in his office," Lacey said. "He said it was the perfect representation of how he saw himself."

"As a lone wolf?" I said.

"Yeah. The ultimate loner. Forced to fend for himself and spend life on the periphery, never completely trusted by anyone."

"The poor baby," Josie said, shaking her head. "Anybody who messed around with those animals the way he did deserved to spend his life alone." She focused on Lacey. "What the heck did you see in the guy?"

"It took some time before I figured out how…misguided Jeremy was," Lacey said with a shrug.

"Misguided? The guy was a nutjob."

"Not at first," Lacey said. "At least, I didn't see it. But as soon as I did, I got away from him as fast as I could."

"Did the cops find anything useful in his journal?" Rooster said.

"Not really," I said. "Detective Williams had a tech with a science background take a look at it. But it's just a collection of drawings, some formulas, a bunch of different quotes, and a lot of rambling passages about mankind's need to conquer the future."

"Conquer the future?" Rooster said.

"Yeah, it's a theme that runs through the journal," I said, then focused on Lacey. "Does that make any sense to you?"

"Not any more than Jeremy's other theories," she said, shaking her head. "He had a bunch of them. Aliens living among us, secret government conspiracies, the evils of fluoride in the water supply. Name the subject, he had a crazy opinion about it."

"I can't believe he didn't have a ton of stuff written down about his work with the hybrids," I said, the question again forcing its way to the surface and tormenting me like a nagging tooth. "It seems counterintuitive to the way the guy operated."

"It is," Lacey said. "Jeremy was meticulous about writing things down."

"Maybe he decided to get rid of it," Rooster said. "He might have realized at some point he'd hit a dead end and tossed it in the fireplace."

"I'm not sure I agree with you, Rooster," Josie said. "There are several generations of hybrids caged up out back. That doesn't sound like a dead end to me."

"On the surface, maybe not," Rooster said. "But who knows what his real goals were? Maybe he just gave up at some point."

"And burned his research notes in a fit of rage?" I said, frowning.

"Stranger things have happened," Rooster said, protesting.

"Yeah, but I still find it hard to believe," I said.

"Lots of times the truth surprises you," he said. "One thing I've learned the hard way is that it's easy to miss simple truths. Sometimes it's hiding in plain sight."

"Yeah, I suppose you're right," I said softly, rocking back and forth on my heels as I looked around the room. My eyes landed on the wolf painting, and I studied it closely. Then my neurons surged and I flinched.

"Don't do that," Josie said. "You're gonna scare the kid."

"What did you just say, Rooster?"

"I said sometimes the truth is hiding in plain sight. What about it?"

"Give me a hand," I said, approaching the wolf painting.

"You want a round of applause?" Josie said as she eyed the appetizer tray.

"Funny," I said, motioning for Rooster to grab one side of the painting. "Let's take this down."

"I take it back," Rooster said to Josie. "She is weird."

"Lift," I said, grabbing the other side. Moments later, we gently set the painting down on the floor. I glanced at the spot on the wall where the painting had been hanging and frowned. "Dang it. I thought I was onto something."

"You expected to find a wall safe?" Rooster said.

"Yeah."

"Well, it was worth a shot," he said, reaching for the painting. "Let's put it back."

"Can't win them all," I said, then had another thought. "Hang on. Turn it around."

Rooster turned the painting around and leaned it against the wall.

"How did you do that?" he said, stunned.

"Lucky guess," I said, staring at two envelopes that were sticking out of a makeshift pocket folder on the back of the painting. I grabbed both envelopes and made my way back to the couch.

"That was spooky," Lacey said, staring at me in disbelief.

"You'll get used to it," Josie said. "What have you got there, Snoopmeister?"

"The thick one is called Understanding the Wolfdog Hybrid," I said, exploring the contents of the thick manila envelope. The other one is sealed."

"What does he have to say about the hybrids?" Josie said, sitting down next to me.

"It looks like he was working on a book," I said, flipping through the pages. "And all his daily logs are here. Diet, feeding times, socialization habits. It's pretty comprehensive."

"That's the Jeremy I knew," Lacey said.

"The book has a lengthy preamble," I said, beginning to read aloud from the first page. "The practice of crossbreeding wolfs with dogs has existed for years, and little is known about the genetic composition of the offspring produced by this breeding practice. I hope this book will both educate and enlighten readers of the benefits and potential dangers associated with this emerging science."

"Science?" Josie said. "Maybe if the guy's name was Dr. Frankenstein."

"He talks a lot about first generation puppies and uses a jelly bean analogy," I said.

"I could go for some jelly beans," Josie said.

"You had more than enough at Halloween to last you a lifetime," I said.

"Hey, it wasn't my fault the trick or treat traffic was light."

"Listen to this," I said, again reading from the document. "If you're breeding a purebred wolf with a purebred dog, you can logically assume both parents have a one hundred percent lineage from a DNA perspective. As an example, put one hundred red jelly beans in a jar to represent the wolf and another hundred green jelly beans to represent the dog's DNA. Select any fifty beans from each jar to represent fifty percent, shared parentage. Since only one color of bean is associated with each parent, all first-generation offspring will logically be a fifty-fifty combination of wolf and dog. But it's the subsequent generations of offspring where the randomness of hybrid DNA combinations come into play."

"I can't believe you dated the guy," Josie said to Lacey.

"I'd never met anyone like him before," she said. "There's something to be said for that."

"I'll take your word for it," Josie said, shaking her head. "What else does he have to say?"

"It gets pretty technical in a hurry," I said, flipping through the document. "He rambles on about nucleotide polymorphisms, Bayesian something or other, outlier genes, and various multivariate factors. And he mentions homozygosity several times. What the heck is that?"

Josie and Lacey glanced at each other then shrugged.

"I must have missed that class," Josie said.

"I've heard the term before," Lacey said. "But I don't have a clue what it means."

"Homozygosity deals with someone who possesses two identical forms of a particular gene," Rooster said. "One inherited from each parent."

"Really?" I said, frowning.

"Hey, I read."

Lacey laughed and patted Rooster on the knee. She left her hand there, and I glanced at Josie and grinned at her before refocusing on the document.

"He's got all the hybrids identified," I said, studying a diagram. "It lists all their names and ages by cage and percentage of wolf for each one. We were right. The two males are purebred wolves. Let's head outside and see how they respond to their names."

"Good call," Josie said. "But let's take a look at the second envelope first."

"Geez, I almost forgot," I said, tearing the seal and removing a stapled document that only had a handful of pages. I flipped through it as I scanned the contents then shook my head. "Wow. What do you know?"

"What is it?" Josie said, peering over my shoulder.

"It's a handwritten copy of Peters' last will and testament," I said with a blank stare.

"Let me see that," Rooster said, reaching for it. He spent a few minutes examining it then handed it to Lacey. "If it's any consolation, he definitely wanted you to have this place."

"Take a look at the last page," I said.

"What about it?" Lacey said.

"Did Peters sign it?" Rooster said.

"He did," Lacey said, nodding. "And it's witnessed as well."

"Now, that's interesting," he said. "Who was it?"

"Clarissa George."

Chapter 19

The closer my due date got, the more the house dogs hovered around me. And it had become readily apparent that my daughter, in addition to the women who would soon be central in her life, was going to have four furry, four-legged protectors keeping a watchful eye over her. As such, Chef Claire's Goldens were curled up at my feet under the desk with Chloe tucked between them. Captain, Josie's Newfie, without enough room to get comfortable, had opted for the couch and was currently stretched out, snoring contentedly.

I took several sips of coffee between stifled yawns and focused on the door when I heard the soft knock.

"Come on in."

All four dogs stirred and got up to greet my visitors. Chief Abrams and Detective Williams responded with head scratches and tummy rubs until the dogs resumed their resting places.

"Thanks for coming over," I said, motioning for them to sit down. "I couldn't bear the thought of trying to climb into the SUV."

"No problem," the Chief said. "Where's Josie?"

"She's doing an annual exam. She said she was going to swing by when she finishes up."

"You look tired," the Chief said. "Did the baby keep you up all night?"

"No, these did," I said, removing the two envelopes we'd found yesterday from a desk drawer. "I was up most of the night reading."

Both men leaned forward and stared at them.

"We found them yesterday out at Cabot Lodge."

"Well, don't keep us in suspense," the Chief said.

"The thick one is all of Peters' research and writing on his work breeding hybrids," I said, then paused for effect. "The other one is Peters' handwritten last will and testament."

"What?" Detective Williams said, reaching for the envelope and removing the document.

"Yeah, it caught us by surprise, too."

"Where did you find them?" the Chief said.

"Behind a painting he had hanging on a wall in the living room," I said, stifling another yawn.

"Huh," Detective Williams grunted. He set the will down on the desk in front of him and frowned.

"What's the matter?" the Chief said, reaching for the document.

"It was witnessed," Detective Williams said. "Last page."

The Chief flipped to the page, and his expression soon matched the detective's confused look.

"He had his research assistant witness it?" the Chief said.

"But she didn't say a word about it during the reading of the will," Detective Williams said.

"No, she didn't," I said. "But in the handwritten version, Peters didn't leave her a book worth a hundred thousand."

"You think she was somehow involved in changing the will?" Detective Williams said.

"Either that, or she was just seizing the opportunity to get her hands on a first-edition copy of The Origin of Species."

"By playing dumb and keeping her mouth shut?" the Chief said, giving it some serious thought.

"Yeah," I said. "But if she was involved in changing the will, that probably means she was part of the murder."

"I gotta tell you," Detective Williams said. "I've been involved in some weird investigations, but this one is off the charts."

"Did you get a chance to interview all the beneficiaries again?" I said.

"We did," the detective said. "That's eight hours of my life I'll never get back."

"Is the wife still making noise about suing Larry?" I said.

"That's the least of Larry's concerns at the moment," Detective Williams said. "She's forcing our hand about arresting him for Peters' murder."

"And you're going along with it?" I said.

"I don't have any choice, Suzy," he said. "Given the evidence in front of us, if she starts squawking to my higherups, which is something she's threatened to do, I'll have some serious problems to deal with."

"Even though he didn't do it?" I said, pressing the point.

"Pretty much," Detective Williams said. "Hopefully, it will sort itself out long before Larry goes to trial."

"When are you going to arrest him?"

"Probably sometime later on today," Detective Williams said. "I called Judge Thompson and explained the situation, but he pretty much confirmed what I already knew. But he thinks Larry will be able to make bail."

"Will things change when you tell them about the handwritten copy?" I said.

"Apart from maybe identifying this woman, Clarissa, as a co-conspirator, I doubt it."

"What did the brother have to say for himself?" I said.

"P-Squared?" Detective Williams said, laughing. "About what you'd expect from an inveterate gambler. He said he and his brother were never close. It sounded like Peters used to help him out from time to time, but he cut P-Squared off several years ago."

"Motive?" I said.

"Sure," the detective said. "He hated his brother."

"Alibi?"

"Said he was playing poker with his buddies in Vegas. A three-day marathon."

"Will it check out?"

"Given the social circle the guy travels in, I doubt if he's going to have a hard time getting people to confirm it," Detective Williams said. "All he'd need to do is sprinkle a little cash around."

"Do you like him for it?" I said.

"Peters' murder? Nah, I'm still leaning toward the wife."

"Does she have an alibi?" I said.

"She was on a Caribbean cruise," Detective Williams said. "Airtight."

"Unless she had a *reeeeally* long piece of firewood, right?" the Chief said, then caught the looks we were giving him. "Well, I liked it."

"Yeah, good one, Chief," I said. "But if she had somebody doing her dirty work, I can still make it work."

"Me too," Detective Williams said. "And since she stands to inherit everything now that the will is invalid, I like her even more for it."

I stared off with a deep frown.

"What is it?" the detective said.

"It seems too easy," I said, then a thought popped. "Hey, I forgot to ask. Did you finally tell Larry about Althea?"

"We did," Chief Abrams said. "He was crushed. Genuinely crushed."

"I feel bad for the guy," I said. "Just when it looks like he's starting to turn his life around, everything falls apart."

"Well, if the wife and brother were working with Althea, that means three people were involved. And you know what they say about the chances three people can keep a secret."

"It's possible, but only if two of them are dead?" I said.

"That's the one," Detective Williams said, then shrugged. "Well, if that was how it went down, we are down to two."

"Maybe P-Squared should be sleeping with one eye open," I said. "What did Charles Howard have to say for himself?"

"Not much," the detective said. "He insists he was simply one of Peters' investors in his wolf research."

"But why would anybody throw millions into breeding hybrids?" I said.

"Howard says it's important work," the Chief said. "He kept prattling on about how it was vital to restoring natural habitats and indigenous species. Calls himself a bleeding-heart environmentalist."

"Did you believe him?"

"Not a word," the Chief said. "He's a strange dude. I understand why he and Peters hit it off."

"Did you ask him how he felt about the possibility of losing control over Peters operating fund?" I said.

"We did," Detective Williams said. "It was like water off a duck's back. It barely registered with him."

"Who the heck doesn't worry about losing control over millions of dollars?" I said.

"Probably somebody with billions," the Chief said. "He said he was happy for Charlotte. Said she deserved to maintain her New York lifestyle. But I think he was lying."

"You think they have history?" I said. "You know, of a romantic nature?"

"I don't think so," Detective Williams said. "Based on what we observed, he seems to be a connoisseur of younger women."

"We interviewed him over lunch at C's," the Chief said. "And he was hitting on every woman in the place under the age of thirty."

"Maybe he's working with Clarissa," I said. "She certainly fits the bill."

"That thought crossed our minds," the Chief said. "But we haven't been able to connect them."

"Howard could have met her at Peters' office," I said.

"It's certainly possible," Detective Williams said. "But I still like the wife for it. And even if she and Howard weren't romantically involved, they may have some shared interest in making sure Peters got removed from the equation."

"Equation, huh?" I said, laughing. "I see what you did there, Detective Williams."

"You two must be rubbing off on me."

"What did you find out about Howard's businesses?" I said.

"That's where it gets tricky," Detective Williams said. "He's got a bunch of different companies."

"Lots of people do," I said, frowning. "What's tricky about it?"

"They're all registered in the Cayman Islands," he said. "I'm sure his holdings are like a spider web."

"The Cayman Islands?" I said.

"Yeah, do you have any idea how complicated that place is when it comes to people who are trying to keep their finances from prying eyes?"

"I could probably ballpark it."

"Huh. Now, there's an idea," the Chief said, nodding at me. "Are you thinking what I am?"

"I'd be surprised if I wasn't."

"What are you talking about?" Detective Williams said.

"Gerald," I said. "You met him at my wedding."

"I did?"

"Yeah, he's the Premier of the Cayman Islands," I said, my neurons surging.

"Which one was he?"

"He was sitting at my mother's table during the reception."

"The big black guy with the booming laugh?" Detective Williams said.

"That's him," I said, nodding.

"That guy runs the government of the Cayman Islands?"

"He certainly does."

"Wow, I thought he was just some guy you and your mom knew."

"He is," I said. "He's a good friend who happens to be the head of the government."

"Do you think he'd be willing to help us out?" the Chief said.

"There's only one way to find out," I said, reaching for my phone.

"You have the Premier of the Cayman Islands on speed dial?" Detective Williams said.

"Sure," I said, making the call. I put the phone on speaker and set it down on the desk. He answered on the third ring. "Hi, Gerald."

"Suzy. Let me guess, you're calling to tell me you just gave birth to the most beautiful little girl on the planet."

"I wish," I said, rubbing my belly. "But it won't be long."

"I can't wait to meet her," Gerald said. "We've missed you down here this winter."

"We missed you too. But we'll be back in full swing next year. Have you got a minute?"

"For you? Of course. What do you need?"

"We're trying to get a handle on the activities of someone who might be involved in a murder," I said.

"A murder? What is it with you and people getting killed?" he said, then followed it with his trademark laugh that reverberated around the office.

"We probably don't want to turn that rock over, Gerald," I said, laughing along. "Anyway, the guy we're looking at apparently has a bunch of companies registered down there."

"It's been known to happen," Gerald said. "And?"

"And I was wondering if you could do a little poking around for us," I said, gently tossing the idea out. "I know it's a lot to ask given how busy you are."

"Geez, Suzy. I'm sure I don't have to tell you how many companies there are down here. And some of the corporate structures are very complex."

"I understand, Gerald. I truly do. But if you could do me just this one tiny favor, I'd be in your debt forever."

"I think we both know that's not true," he said, laughing again. "But nice try."

"Please."

"Do you really think this guy might have killed someone?" Gerald said.

"We think it's a distinct possibility," I said.

"We?"

"Oh, I probably should have mentioned that I'm here with Chief Abrams and Detective Williams from the state police."

"Hi, Gerald," the Chief said.

"Hey, Chief. How's it going?" Gerald said. "Detective Williams. I think we met at the wedding, right?"

"We did," the detective said. "We'd really appreciate any help you could give us, sir."

"Sir?" Gerald said. "How official."

"I wasn't going to presume familiarity, sir," Detective Williams said.

"You really need to make a trip to the Islands, Detective," Gerald said. "A week down here will knock that right out of you."

"I'll keep that in mind, Premier."

"Okay, Suzy. I'll play. But it's gonna cost you at least two dinners. One at the restaurant. And a barbecue at your mom's place."

"And a box of Cubans, right?"

"You know me so well. What's the guy's name?"

"Charles Howard," I said.

A lengthy silence ensued, and I exchanged confused looks with both cops as we waited it out.

"You still there, Gerald?"

"I am," he whispered. "Did you say Charles Howard?"

"Here we go," I said. "Touched a nerve, huh?"

"You did indeed," Gerald said.

"Who is he?"

"He's one of my biggest campaign contributors."

"Really? What does he do?"

"You mean, apart from throw money at me?"

"Yeah. Apart from that."

"I have no idea," Gerald said. "I know he has a web of companies registered down here, but I've only met him a few times."

"You barely know him, and he just decided to give you a bunch of money?" I said, confused.

"He's one of those guys who consider political contributions part of the ongoing cost of doing business," Gerald said. "I love those guys."

"I'm sure you do," I said, grinning at both cops. Then I had an idea. "How would it play in the press if word got out one of your biggest contributors was involved in a murder?"

"You read my mind," Gerald said. "At a minimum, it would be a major distraction."

"But if it got out that you helped law enforcement officials over here apprehend a dangerous criminal, I can see all sorts of ways you could spin that to your advantage."

"I do like the way your brain works," Gerald said. "Okay, when do you need the information?"

"As soon as possible."

"I'll be in touch as soon as I have something."

"Thanks, Gerald. I really appreciate it."

"I know you do," he said. "And that's one of the reasons I'm willing to help."

"You're a good friend."

"Just remember to tell that to the reporters when they call you," he said.

"You think they're going to call?"

"Unless my press secretary wants to start looking for another job, they better," he said, then ended the call with another booming laugh.

"Okay," I said, glancing back and forth at them. "What's next?"

"The wife said during her interview she wanted to get a look at Cabot Lodge," Detective Williams said.

I gave his comment some thought then nodded when my neurons flared.

"What a good idea. Actually, I think all the beneficiaries should see the place," I said.

"How do you plan on making that happen?" Detective Williams said.

"By inviting them all out for a dinner party."

"What are you gonna serve?" the Chief said.

"No idea," I said. "But I'm sure Chef Claire will think of something."

Chapter 20

With spoons at the ready, Josie and I hovered near the stove where Chef Claire was putting the final touches on a large pot of soup. She added a splash of brandy, about half a cup of cream then stirred it with a wooden spoon. She leaned over the pot, took a sniff then nodded to herself. She glanced over and laughed at our expressions.

"You look like you haven't eaten in a week," she said, shaking her head. "Go ahead. Give it a taste and let me know if it needs anything."

"It's so green," Josie said as she stared into the pot.

"Well, that tends to happen when you use a lot of peas and spinach," Chef Claire said.

"Everyone's a comedian," Josie said, gently nudging Chef Claire to one side.

We both sampled a spoonful and savored it. I looked at Josie who beamed back.

"It's incredible, Chef Claire," I said. "Bacon?"

"Close," she said. "I went with the jamón ibérico."

"Expensive soup," I said.

"I had some I wanted to use up," Chef Claire said, then fixed a stare on Josie. "And I could have sworn we had more left."

"Probably mice," Josie said, slicing off the end piece of a loaf of rustic Italian. "Now for the real challenge. How well does this soup hold up to the dunk test?" Josie turned back toward the stove and dropped the piece of bread on the floor. She bent down and picked it up.

"Josie," Chef Claire said, her voice rising in warning. "I swear, if you try to dunk that piece of bread in my soup after it's been on the floor, I'm going to hit you with my bat."

"Hey, it's not like I've got a communicable disease," Josie said. "Besides, who would ever know?"

"I would," Chef Claire said.

"Then I'll just drizzle a spoonful of soup over the bread," Josie said.

"Not until you get a clean spoon," Chef Claire said.

"Yes, Commandant."

"You brought your bat?" I said, grabbing a clean spoon of my own.

"You said I might be cooking dinner for a killer," Chef Claire said with a shrug.

"Among others," I said, then savored another spoonful. "God, that's so good. The mint and brandy are a great combo."

"Thanks," Chef Claire said. "Does it need anything?"

"Just a spot in the Culinary Hall of Fame," Josie said, exhaling. "I'd be happy with just the soup and bread." Then she beamed at Chef Claire. "But I know you have more up your sleeve. What's the main course?"

"Beef Wellington."

"Really?" I said. "I can't remember the last time you made that."

"Yeah, I can't either," Chef Claire said. "But I've been thinking about doing a retro-night at the restaurant once a week this summer. You know, bring back some of the old classics. So, I thought I should start brushing up."

"My mother's going to love it."

"It was her idea," Chef Claire said. "Is she coming tonight?"

"No, she and Paulie are spending a couple days in Toronto."

Rooster entered the kitchen and approached the stove.

"May I?" he said.

Chef Claire handed him a spoon, and he sampled the soup.

"You're a genius, Chef Claire."

"Aren't you sweet. Where's Lacey?"

"She's outside feeding the hybrids," Rooster said. "So, what's the game plan for tonight?"

"I thought we'd go with one of the classics," I said.

"Feed them well, give them lots of wine then sit back and wait for them to start talking?" Rooster said.

"Pretty much," I said, then turned to Josie. "Let's go see if Lacey needs a hand."

"Good idea," Josie said. "Just a sec. I've got a question for Rooster."

"Here we go," he said, raising an eyebrow.

"What's going on with you two?"

"Is that really any of your business?"

"Hey, if I waited until things were my business, I'd never get a question in."

"Let's say we're still working our way through the situation and leave it at that."

"You're no fun," Josie said, gently punching him on the shoulder as she headed for the door.

I followed Josie outside onto the porch and grabbed the railing as I began slowly working my way down the steps.

"Take your time," Josie said, keeping a close eye on me.

"I'm fine," I said, then stopped halfway down the steps to catch my breath. "I can't wait for this to be over."

"It won't be long. Just take your time and keep breathing."

We reached the bottom step, and I looked around. The snow was gone, and the grass was showing signs of green. But the wind was up. I zipped my jacket as we headed for the row of cages. Lacey was pushing chunks of raw meat through the slots in each cage.

"You know what this reminds me of?" Josie said.

"What are you talking about?"

"The way Lacey is shoving food through those slots. It reminds me of dinnertime at a maximum-security prison."

"Actually, that's pretty close," I said, coming to a stop at the first cage where the male wolf inside was staring back at me. I took a step closer, and the wolf growled and bared its teeth. I checked the notes I'd made when I read Peters' research notes. "His name is Thelonious. He's five. Peters got him from a farmer in Wyoming."

"Let me guess, the farmer caught the wolf trying to kill his cattle," Josie said, studying the animal who continued to bare its teeth at us.

"Yeah, wolves can be a problem out there," I said.

"Thelonious? Strange name."

"The male in the next cage is called Miles. Peters must have been a jazz fan."

We caught up with Lacey who was standing outside the last cage and trying to get a look at the litter of puppies who were still huddled together in the doghouse structure.

"Hi, guys," she said, finally noticing our presence.

"Hey," Josie said, nodding at the puppies. "How are they doing?"

"I think they're doing fine," Lacey said. "But there's no way mama is going to let us get a closer look."

"What did Peters say about the litter?" Josie said.

"Fourth-generation. He was hoping the puppies would fall somewhere between twenty-five and thirty percent wolf," I said, checking my notes.

"That's way too high for any chance they could be socialized," Lacey said, shaking her head.

"Yeah, there's no way," I said, depressed by the thought of what was ahead for the puppies.

"What are we going to do with them?" Lacey said.

"No idea," I said, shaking my head.

"Well, step one is keeping the widow's hands off them," Josie said.

"It shouldn't be that hard," I said with a grin. "Chef Claire did bring her bat."

"Now there's an idea," Josie said.

"What?" Lacey said.

"Nothing," Josie said. "Can we give you a hand with anything?"

"No, thanks. I'm pretty much done. Have our guests arrived?"

"Not yet," I said as we all headed back toward the lodge.

"Do you need me to do anything tonight?" Lacey said.

"Just be yourself and play it by ear," I said.

"Don't worry," Josie deadpanned. "Rooster will be there to protect you."

Lacey blushed, then looked over at us.

"Is it that obvious?"

"It's a little hard to miss," Josie said.

"He's an amazing man," Lacey said.

"No argument from us," I said. "Are you worried about the age difference?"

"I was," Lacey said. "But less so on a daily basis."

"Word of advice," I said, unable to stop the memory from returning. "Enjoy each day. Because you never know."

Josie squeezed my hand affectionately as she led me up the steps. We found Chef Claire and Rooster chatting in the kitchen.

"All set?" Rooster said.

"They're all fed and watered," Lacey said, peering into the pot of soup. "Smells fantastic."

"It should be edible," Chef Claire said. "Okay, we need to set the table. How many are coming?"

I did the math in my head.

"Well, let's see. Counting the five of us, the Chief and Detective Williams, and four beneficiaries, eleven."

"Good job," Josie said. "You didn't even have to take a shoe off."

"Shut it."

"Have you seen the dining room?" Lacey said. "It's amazing."

"Yeah, I snuck a peek at it earlier," Chef Claire said. "This must have been quite a place in the old days."

"I could do without the animal heads," Lacey said. "They're enough to make you lose your appetite."

"Not a chance," Josie said, grabbing a stack of dishes.

Chapter 21

The dining room in question was straight out of the 1950s. Dark mahogany dominated and an overhead chandelier and several stained-glass lamps provided an eerie glow that could have been the set from a classic movie. The dinner table sat two dozen easily, and the tabletop appeared to be constructed from a single piece of wood that had to be thirty feet long. The overall setting was a bit odd, but the room worked, and the entire group seemed content as we worked our way through the meal. Charlotte, the widow, set her utensils down on her empty plate then took a long sip of wine. Her eyes settled on Chef Claire.

"What are you doing hiding out in the hinterlands?" she said. "With your skills, you should be in New York."

"I am in New York," Chef Claire said, then slid the last piece of beef wellington into her mouth.

"I mean the *real* New York," Charlotte said. "Not this upstate wasteland."

"Wasteland?" I whispered.

"Let it go," Josie said, patting my hand.

"You really should think about opening another restaurant," Charlotte said, pressing the point.

"We already have another restaurant," Chef Claire said with a shrug then reached for her wine.

"Really? Where?" Charlotte said.

"The Cayman Islands," Chef Claire said.

"The C's on Grand Cayman is your restaurant?" Charles Howard said, surprised.

"It is," Chef Claire said. "Actually, there's four of us that own both of them."

"I eat there every time I'm on the island," Charles Howard said.

"Most people do," Josie said.

"You do that amazing grilled Dorado."

"That's us," Chef Claire said, nodding.

"Dorado?" P-Squared said.

"Mahi-mahi," Charles Howard said. "That's what they call it down there."

"Do you visit Cayman a lot?" I said, seizing the opening.

"A couple times a year."

"On business?" I said, going for casual.

"A bit of both," he said.

"We have a place down there," I said, patting my belly. "But for obvious reasons, we didn't get down this winter."

I was about to press forward when Charlotte reentered the conversation. Miffed, I sat back and waited out the interruption.

"You really should think about opening a restaurant in New York," she said, leaning forward with her elbows on the table.

"Why would we want to do that?" Chef Claire said between sips of wine.

"To get your name out there. Continue to build your reputation," Charlotte said.

"Nah, plenty of people know who I am."

"Then how about to make a lot of money?"

"I already make more than enough," Chef Claire said. "And I can't spend what I make now."

"Obviously," Charlotte said with a laugh. "You aren't trying hard enough."

"I think I'll pass, Charlotte," Chef Claire said. "But thanks for thinking of me."

Lacey caught my eye, and I returned her look with a slight nod. Lacey glanced around the table then tossed back what was left in her wine glass.

"Okay, who's ready for a tour?" she said, getting to her feet.

"I can't wait to see the place," Charles said.

"What a good idea," I said, using both hands to push myself up from the table. "After the tour, we'll have coffee and dessert in front of the fire."

"Works for me," P-Squared said, pushing his chair back from the table.

Charlotte, along with Charles Howard and Clarissa, got up and followed Lacey out of the dining room. At the door, Clarissa stopped and turned back to us.

"You want some help with the dishes?" she said.

"No, you guys go ahead," I said. "We've got it under control."

I waited until I heard the sound of footsteps going up the stairs then focused on the collection of dirty dishes on the table.

"Wine glasses," I said in a low voice. "Make sure to grab them by the stems." I turned to Detective Abrams. "Did you remember to bring some evidence bags?"

"What am I, an idiot?" he said, rolling his eyes at me.

"Sorry," I said. "Let's do it in the kitchen. Rooster, do you mind keeping an eye out for them?"

"You got it," he said, heading into the kitchen.

We all followed and quickly put the wine glasses into plastic bags. Detective Williams sealed them then jotted the names on the outside in magic marker.

"You think you'll find anything new about them?" Josie said, picking at a corner of the chocolate torte sitting on the counter. Then she flinched and grabbed her hand. "Ow. Hey, knock it off."

"Don't pick at the cake with your fingers," Chef Claire said as she waved a wooden spoon at the cake thief. "What is wrong with you?"

"Consider it an homage to your culinary skills," Josie said as she continued to rub her hand. "Man, that hurt."

"Good."

From the door, Rooster coughed loudly, and we all spotted P-Squared come to a stop next to him.

"I thought I might take a glass of wine with me," he said.

"Sure," Chef Claire said, pouring a glass and handing it to him.

He took a sip and lingered in the doorway.

"Can I get you something else?" Chef Claire said.

"No, this is fine, thanks," P-Squared said, glancing back and forth at both cops.

"Something on your mind, Peter?" Detective Williams said, staring back.

"If you don't mind, I prefer P-Squared, Detective. It's kind of my calling card."

"Sorry. What can we do for you?"

"I was just wondering which one of us you guys think killed Jeremy," he said, leaning against the doorjamb.

"What makes you think we suspect any of you?" Detective Williams said.

"Let's call it a hunch," P-Squared said, then forced a small laugh. "You bring us way out here in the wilderness. To the actual crime scene, no less."

"Charlotte mentioned she wanted to see the place," Chief Abrams said. "We thought the rest of you might want to check it out. And eat Chef Claire's food in the process."

"Okay," he said, again glancing back and forth at the cops. "If you say so. But I can't shake the feeling this would be the perfect spot to get a reaction out of whoever killed Jeremy."

"Did you come up with that all by yourself?" Josie said.

"Actually, Charlotte might have mentioned it on the drive over," he said, then drained his wine and held his glass out for a refill. Chef Claire obliged, and he took another sip. He remained propped up against the doorjamb, his eyes half-closed. "Great dinner."

"Thanks," Chef Claire said.

"Is there something else you need?" Detective Williams said.

"Actually, there is," P-Squared said. "I was wondering if there's a casino around here?"

"Yeah, there are," Chief Abrams said. "But it's a two-hour drive to any of them."

"Indian casinos, right?"

"They are," the Chief said.

"I've never had any luck at them," P-Squared said. "I think they're rigged. You know, against outsiders."

We all stared at him and waited for him to continue.

"Yeah, I think they're rigged as some sort of payback for what we did to them."

"Score one for the Native Americans," Josie said.

"Well, what can you do, right?" P-Squared said more to himself than anyone else. "But I'm jonesing to play some poker. I think I'll check it out."

"But not tonight, right?" the Chief said, nodding at the man's wine glass.

"What? Oh, got it. No, not tonight," P-Squared said with a grin. "The last thing I need is another DUI. Okay, time to join the tour."

We watched him head off and waited until Rooster gave us the all clear signal.

"What a waste of oxygen," Josie said, massaging her knuckles.

"What did you ask me before P-Squared honored us with his presence?" Detective Williams said.

"I asked if you thought the fingerprint analysis would uncover anything," Josie said.

"It might," Detective Williams said. "We took a look at all of them in our system, but nothing useful came back."

"What are you looking for?" Chef Claire said.

"Criminal records. Aliases and prior lives, stuff like that," I said, then turned to Detective Williams. "How long will it take to run the analysis?"

"It depends," he said. "Anywhere from a week to a couple of months."

"A couple of months?" I said with a scowl. "That's ridiculous."

"It is what it is," the detective said.

"You're going philosophical on me?"

"Hey, I'm just explaining how things work."

"Or don't work."

"Well, I don't know what to tell you, Suzy," he said. "Unless you have some serious juice with the FBI, we're just going to have to wait."

The penny dropped, and I beamed at both cops.

"Actually, I do," I said, glancing at Chef Claire. "Agent Tompkins. He owes me a favor."

"Not a bad idea," Chief Abrams said. "But what if he's too busy or refuses to help?"

"Then we'll just have Chef Claire ask him," I said. "He *luuuvs* Chef Claire."

Josie snorted.

"Don't start," Chef Claire said, brandishing the wooden spoon.

I grinned at her, then headed back into the dining room to make the call. A few minutes later, I returned and nodded.

"He'll do it," I said. "But we'll need to get the glasses down to the FBI office in Buffalo."

"I can get one of my guys to drive them down in the morning," Detective Williams said. "Did he say how long it would take?"

"A couple of days, maybe sooner," I said, then turned to Chef Claire. "Agent Tompkins says hi."

234

"How's he doing?"

"He sounded good," I said. "Oh, by the way, you're going to have to cook him dinner next time he's in town. And he also mentioned something about taking you to a movie."

"I live to serve," Chef Claire deadpanned.

"I'm just doing my part to push the relationship along," I said with a laugh. "Okay, we've got Gerald working on the Cayman connection. And the FBI is running the fingerprint analysis. What's next?"

"I think we should try to get them talking about themselves," Detective Williams said. "Especially the wife."

"And Clarissa," Chief Abrams said. "She's been hitting the wine hard and is getting chatty."

"But not Charles," Josie said. "He's a bit of a cold fish."

"I think he's just being cautious," I said.

"About what?" Josie said.

"If I knew that, we wouldn't need to get him talking."

"There's no need to get snarky."

"What about the brother?" Chef Claire said. "P-Squared. He's weird."

"He's a follower," Detective Williams said. "And if he is involved in some way, I'm willing to bet he's taking orders from somebody else."

"What are you serving with dessert?" I said to Chef Claire.

"Port."

"Portuguese?" I said.

"No, I went Australian. The Penfolds Grandfather."

"Ah, family," Josie said. "It's going to go great with that torte."

"Perfect," I said to Chef Claire. "Let's see if we can get a couple of bottles down them."

"Got it. Heavy-handed house pour it is," Chef Claire said. "But it's got some kick and sneaks up on you. Who's driving home later?"

"I am," Chief Abrams said. "The sacrifices I make."

"We'll send a bottle home with you, Chief," Chef Claire said. "Okay, who's ready for dessert?"

Chapter 22

"Would anyone like another slice of torte?" Chef Claire said, glancing around the group.

"Oh, my. No, thank you," Charlotte said. "I couldn't possibly eat another bite. But I will have some more port if you don't mind."

Chef Claire refilled her glass then topped off the others.

"Do you eat like this all the time?" Charlotte said.

"Pretty much," Chef Claire said. "We like good food."

"Well, that dinner certainly qualified," Charles Howard said. "Well done. Well done, indeed."

"Thank you," Chef Claire said, raising her glass in salute.

"How did you and Jeremy cross paths, Charles?" I said.

"He spoke at a venture capitalist conference I was at," Charles Howard said.

"When was that?"

"Let's see," he said, searching his memory bank. "It must have been six, maybe seven years ago."

"It was seven," Charlotte said. "I remember because it was right around the time he left New York."

"Why did he leave?" I said.

"To get away from me, obviously," she said, glaring at Lacey.

"You must have someone else in mind, Charlotte," Lacey said, returning the stare. "I met Jeremy four years ago."

"I must be thinking of someone else," Charlotte said, then let loose with a bitter laugh. "But who could keep them straight? There were so many."

"Jeremy was looking for venture capital?" I said to Charles.

"He was. For his research with the hybrids."

"Why would anybody throw VC money at a project like that?" Detective Williams said.

"He was convinced his research had wider applications," Charles Howard said with a shrug.

I gave his comment some thought, then frowned when a question emerged.

"Human application?" I said.

"Of course," Charles Howard said.

"How could playing around with wolf and dog genetics possibly have human application?" Josie said.

238

"Oh, I'm way out of my league when it comes to the actual science involved," he said. "I'm an investor, not a scientist."

"Sure, sure," I said, nodding. "Can I ask how much you invested?"

"At first, only ten million."

"Only ten, huh?" Josie said.

"It's a small price to pay for controlling interest in a supernova," he said, then noticed our confusion. "It's what I call startup ventures that get off the ground and explode with growth."

"What do you call startups that don't?" Josie said.

"Black holes."

"Because you're constantly sinking money into them that just disappears?" I said.

"Well done," Charles said with a laugh. "I use a very straightforward approach. For every ten startups I sink money into, I expect to get nine black holes. But that one supernova more than makes up for it."

"How many companies have you put money into?" Chef Claire said.

"Dozens," he said. "But I usually keep an active roster of five or six at any given time."

"Ten million here, ten million there," Josie said. "Pretty soon you're talking about real money."

"Exactly," he said, nodding as he reached for his glass of port.

"Did Jeremy's research pan out?" I said.

"Apart from being able to control the genetics of those hybrid wolves, not a bit," Charles said.

"A black hole?" I said.

"They don't get much blacker," he said, laughing.

"How much money did you sink into it?" I said.

"Oh, I'd rather not say. It's embarrassing."

"Why did you keep plowing money into it?" Chief Abrams said.

"I had a soft spot for Jeremy," Charles Howard said. "He was so...unique. Truly a remarkable man. Just misguided when it came to what you and I would call normal daily life. Maladjusted is probably the closest term I can come up with."

"You'll get no argument from me," Charlotte said. "What about you, Lacey? Can I assume we agree on at least that?"

"I really don't want to get into it, Charlotte."

"Of course not," Charlotte said with an evil grin before turning to Clarissa. "What about you, dear? How did you handle Jeremy's idiosyncrasies?"

"With kid gloves, usually," Clarissa said, refilling her glass.

"How did you end up working for him?" I said.

"I'd heard about his work, and it sounded interesting," she said, then took a long sip. "I finally worked up the courage to stop by his office. We chatted for about an hour, and I just asked him to hire me."

"What's your academic background?" Lacey said.

"Biology. Biochemistry is more accurate," Clarissa said. "I was planning to start my doctoral work, but I put it on the back burner after I started working for Jeremy."

"Are you going to go back to school?" I said.

"I'm not sure what I'm going to do now," Clarissa said, then glanced back and forth at the two cops. "But there's no need to worry about that until you guys give me the okay to leave town, right?"

"We're very sorry about that, Clarissa," Detective Williams said. "But I'm sure you understand. It's pretty standard procedure."

"Since it's obvious I didn't have anything to do with what happened to Jeremy, I don't know why I can't leave."

"It won't be long," Detective Williams said.

"Chill out, girl," Charlotte said, then giggled as she glanced around. "Did I say that right?"

"I don't know who's worse," Clarissa said. "You or the cops."

"Have another glass of port while you sort it out," Charlotte said.

"I've been wondering something," Lacey said as she turned to Charles Howard right on cue. "Why do you think Jeremy left you control of his operating fund?"

"He didn't," Charlotte said.

"Let's just wait for the lawyers to sort that one out, Charlotte," Charles said. "But to answer your question, I imagine he did it out of guilt."

"For what, wasting millions of your money?" Lacey said.

"That would be my guess," he said. "And he obviously wanted you to continue his research. Maybe he felt he could trust me to provide the ongoing funds needed to do it. As opposed to someone else."

"Stuff a sock in it, Charles," Charlotte snapped.

"You're going to challenge the will?" Lacey said.

"I am," he said. "If it looks like Charlotte might try getting in the way."

"But why?" Clarissa said.

"Because I know that's what Jeremy would have wanted," Charles Howard said, then flashed Charlotte an evil grin.

"But you said yourself you weren't worried about the money," Clarissa said.

"I'm not," Charles said with a shrug. "It's more about the principle involved."

"For the last time," Charlotte said. "There is no will. Thanks to that shyster lawyer."

"Maybe there's another copy of the will floating around," Lacey said casually.

I was ready for her comment and was concentrating on Clarissa's face. She flinched briefly, and I knew Lacey's remark had struck a nerve.

"Another copy of the will?" Charlotte said. "That's all we need."

"Nothing like muddying the water," Clarissa said.

"So, what do you think of Cabot Lodge, Charlotte?" I said.

"It's okay," she said, glancing around the room. "If you're into Early Pioneer. Which I'm not."

"What do you think you're going to do with the place?" I said.

"Sell it," she said as a simple statement of fact. "Just as soon as I get rid of those animals out back."

"Uh, Charlotte," I said. "I need to tell you that you aren't going to be able to do that."

"Do what?"

"Have them put down."

"Really?" she said, draping a leg over her knee. "Watch me."

"Well, since Charles is talking about bringing in a lawyer, we might as well add a few more to the mix, right?"

"Works for me," Josie said, glaring at the widow.

"You're going to sue me?" Charlotte said, raising an eyebrow at me.

"No," I said, shaking my head. "Let's call it an injunction."

"On whose authority?"

"District court," Josie said.

"And the attorney general of New York," I said.

"What?" Charlotte said. "What on earth does the attorney general have to do with this?"

"He's a friend of my mother," I said. "And it turns out, he's quite an animal lover."

"Don't forget the reporter from the New York Times," Chef Claire said.

"Oh, right," I said, grinning at her before turning back to Charlotte. "Do you know a feature writer by the name of Geoffrey Goodwin?"

Charlotte chewed her bottom lip before responding.

"I'm familiar with his work," she said eventually.

"His stuff has a bit of a gossipy flavor to it," I said. "But he's good. And he loves taking shots at socialites who think they're somehow above the fray."

"He'd have a field day with a story about someone who had a bunch of rare animals put down just because they were *inconvenient*," Rooster said.

"Let me guess," Charlotte said. "Goodwin's also a friend of your mother?"

"No, actually he's a friend of mine," Rooster said. "He stores his boat at my marina. And we fish together in the summer."

"Why on earth do you even care about that bunch of creatures?" Charlotte said, genuinely bewildered by the idea.

"Rhetorical?" Josie said, glancing over at me.

"No, I don't think she was going for rhetorical."

"That's what I thought," Josie said, nodding. "Just wanted to make sure."

"It was worth checking, though," I said, then focused on Charlotte. "We care about them because that's what we do."

Charlotte fell silent and looked back and forth at us for a long time before exhaling audibly.

"Okay. What do you want?"

"Just some time," I said. "We simply want to leave the hybrids where they are until we can figure out what to do with them."

"That's it?"

"That's it."

"There must be wolf sanctuaries around they could go to," Charlotte said.

"Maybe the two males," Josie said. "But the hybrids might not last a week living among purebreds."

"Then put them up for adoption," Charlotte said. "People are always looking for exotic pets."

"Too dangerous," I said. "They have enough wolf in them to make them very unpredictable. Especially around young kids."

"So, what you're telling me is that, once again, Jeremy has left a mess behind other people are going to have to clean up?"

"Well, I can't speak to Jeremy's history, but this one is definitely a mess," I said.

"How long will you need?" Charlotte said.

"We really don't know," I said. "But let's start with a month and go from there. It'll take at least that long for the lawyers to sort out the will."

"Okay, I can do that," Charlotte said, getting to her feet. "Now, if you'll excuse me for a few minutes. I need to use the facilities then call my lawyer."

We watched her stagger slightly as she headed down the hall toward the bathroom. Charles Howard shook his head at her then focused on me.

"Well played."

"Thanks," I said. "Actually, it was a group effort."

"Was the part about the reporter from the Times true?" Charles said.

"Yeah," Rooster said. "Geoffrey was all over it."

"I'm sure he was," Charles said. "Is the AG really your mom's buddy?"

"He is."

"And you already called him?" Charles said.

"Nah," I said, shaking my head. "My mom doesn't like to bug him unless it's absolutely necessary."

"So, you were bluffing?"

"Maybe a little."

Chapter 23

Chief Abrams concentrated on his menu as if he were studying for a math test. Josie and I watched him with smiles on our faces then looked up when our server approached.

"Hey, Sherry," I said. "How are you settling in?"

"It's great," she said. "I love it here. Chef Claire is so cool to work for."

"Well, we're glad you're here," Josie said.

"What did you decide on?"

"We're both doing the special," Josie said.

"Special?" the Chief said, finally looking up from his menu. "I didn't think about that. What is it?"

"Tomato soup and grilled cheese," I said. "Comfort food for a cold and rainy day in March."

"Is that the soup with vermouth and gorgonzola?" he said.

"That's the one," Josie said. "And she's started making the grilled cheese with the rustic Italian."

"She tested it out on us at the house last week," I said. "Total knee-buckler."

"I'm in," the Chief said, handing his menu to our server.

"Make it four specials, please," I said. "We're waiting for one more, and I'm sure he'll be happy with it."

"And if he's not, I'll eat it," Josie said.

"You got it," Sherry said, then headed for the kitchen.

"What did Detective Williams have to say?" I said.

"He didn't go into it over the phone," the Chief said. "He only said he had some news we needed to talk about."

"Color me intrigued," I said, taking a sip of club soda. Then I pressed a hand against my belly.

"Somebody kicking up a storm?" Josie said.

"Yeah, she's definitely making her presence known," I said, continuing to gently hold my hand over the area. "It won't be long."

"Which means you need to stay close to home," Josie said.

"Yeah, that's probably a good idea."

Detective Williams entered the dining room, and as soon as he spotted us, he approached and sat down.

"Good afternoon," he said. "What's good today?"

"We ordered you the special," I said. "Soup and a sandwich."

"Is that what you're having?"

"It is."

"Far be it for me to question your ordering abilities." He poured himself a glass of water, took a sip then sat back in his chair. "Your friend at the FBI delivered."

"What did he find?" the Chief said.

"A lot. I'd love to have access to the information those guys do," the detective said. "You know, right at your fingertips." He reached into his bag and removed a notebook. "I took a lot of notes. Let's start with the easy ones and work our way up."

I leaned forward with my elbows on the table.

"Should I make myself scarce?" Josie said.

"Why would you do that?" Detective Williams said.

"Because I'm not a cop."

"Neither am I," I said, glancing at her.

"Really?" Josie deadpanned. "I guess I forget that sometimes."

"Funny."

"Don't worry about it, Josie," Detective Williams said, flipping through the pages in his notebook. "We're way past that."

"Since when?" Josie said.

"Since she figured out the last four murder cases I've been involved in," he said, nodding in my direction. "But if anybody asks, both of you have been added as technical consultants to this investigation."

"Technical consultants?" Josie said, raising an eyebrow.

"The wolf research aspect of the case," the detective said.

"How about that?" she said. "I'm a technical consultant."

"Don't get too excited," I said, laughing. "I'm sure it's a title without a paycheck."

"It's always something, huh?"

"So, what have you got?" I said, focusing on the detective.

"Well, there's nothing on Charles Howard," the detective said. "Either he's a model citizen, or really good at covering his tracks. Have you heard back from the Premier yet?"

"Not yet," I said, shaking my head. "I'm going to give him another day or two before I call."

"That's fine," Detective Williams said. "Based on what I got from Agent Tompkins, I don't think we need to worry about Mr. Howard."

"This must be good," Josie said.

"Okay, here we go," he said, reading from his notes. "P-Squared. Mr. Peter Peters. The stuff I already got from our system is pretty much all there is. Two DUIs. A couple of possession charges and a handful of B&Es. Probably did those to fund his drug habit. But he's been clean for several years."

"That's it?" I said.

"No, there's one the FBI had that we didn't," he said. "An aggravated assault arrest in Vegas."

"So, he does have a violent streak," I said.

"He does. And it gets even better. Guess who filed the charge?"

"His brother," I said without hesitation.

"How did you know that?" Detective Williams said.

"You said it gets better," I said with a shrug. "Who else would we be talking about?"

"If you say so," he said, glancing at the Chief who shrugged back at him. "Anyway, the brothers got into a major fight in Vegas, and P-Squared put him in the hospital. Broken ribs, lacerations, concussion."

"Lovely," Josie said.

"But Jeremy dropped the charges a couple of days later," Detective Williams said. "That's why our system didn't pick it up."

"But the FBI still has the original arrest?" Josie said.

"They do. I doubt if the Feebs even have a delete key on their computers," the detective said.

"What was the fight about?" Josie said.

"Money," I said.

"You reading my notes?" Detective Williams said.

"No, but during the reading of the will, Jeremy took some shots at his brother when he told him he was leaving him a thousand bucks."

"Apparently, Jeremy had gotten tired of funding his brother's gambling habit."

"I smell a motive," the Chief said.

"I smell our lunch," Josie said, doing a half-turn as Sherry arrived carrying a tray.

She set our food in front of us, checked to make sure we had everything we needed, then left. We ate in silence for several moments before Detective Williams glanced up from his soup.

"My mom used to make me tomato soup and grilled cheese whenever I got sick," he said.

"Mine too," Josie said. "But it was nothing like this."

"You got that right," Detective Williams said. "How many different cheeses does she put in this sandwich?"

"Five," I said, taking a big bite. "Did you get anything else?"

"Yeah. A bunch. And it gets better," the detective said, taking another bite of his sandwich. He chewed as he checked his notes then continued. "Charlotte Peters. Art history professor. Museum and gallery consultant. Wannabe New York socialite."

"She's busy," Josie said.

"Been married three times, divorced twice. Now, obviously widowed," Detective Williams said. "Charlotte Smith, Charlotte Carrier, then, of course, Charlotte Peters."

"Does she have a record?" I said.

"Not under any of those names," he said with a coy grin.

I thought about his comment then the penny dropped.

"She changed her identity at some point, didn't she?" I said.

"Very good. Right before her first marriage. She was born Josephine Andrews. We got a match on the prints."

"Let me guess. Josephine Andrews has a criminal record," I said.

"She does. But when Charlotte got her new identity, Josephine Andrews dropped completely off the radar,"

Detective Williams said. "She had multiple arrests as a teenager that continued until she was in her early twenties."

"What for?" Chief Abrams said, then wiped his mouth and leaned forward in his chair.

"Petty theft at first," Detective Williams said. "And then she graduated to more sophisticated scams. She did some stuff with fake credit cards. Then she and a couple of her girlfriends set up a phony escort agency. That's the one that got the FBI's attention because it crossed state lines. They'd set up appointments, then get the johns in a compromising position and take off with their money and jewelry."

"But the johns were too embarrassed to report it, right?" I said.

"Pretty much," Detective Williams said. "And just when the cops were closing in, she disappeared into thin air."

"With her new identity," I said, nodding.

"Then our friend, Charlotte, got married and had a kid," he said. "A daughter. Her first husband paid for her schoolwork, and when Charlotte got her PhD, she dumped the guy and married her second husband. That lasted five years, then she somehow crossed paths with the now deceased Jeremy Peters."

"But she hasn't been in any trouble since she became Charlotte?" the Chief said.

"It doesn't look like it."

"Did she have any more kids?" the Chief said.

"No. Just the one."

"What about Charlotte's daughter? Anything on her?"

"A lot," Detective Williams said. "She was born Prudence Smith."

"Her parents called her Prudence?" Josie said. "No wonder the kid got in trouble."

"Yeah, it was kind of cruel, wasn't it?" Detective Williams said. "The kid was a grifter from the time she was eight-years-old. In and out of juvie multiple times. Theft, drugs, burglary, teenage prostitution, you name it. Apparently, Charlotte finally had enough and disowned her."

"What happened to her?" the Chief said.

"That's the weird part. She dropped off the radar. Just like her mother had earlier."

"She probably changed her name," Josie said. "I know I would have. Prudence? That's just cruel."

"Did the FBI have anything on Clarissa?" I said.

"Not really," Detective Williams said. "She's been working for Peters for a couple of years. Before that, she was in college. She managed to get caught up in some counterfeit art scam while she was in grad school, but the cops couldn't prove she was involved. Interviewed, but never charged. That's all there is on Clarissa."

My neurons surged, and I flinched just before I was about to take a bite of my grilled cheese.

"Here we go," Josie said, staring at me.

"What is it?" the Chief said.

"I'm not sure," I said, rubbing my forehead. "Let's back up a bit. What was Prudence's full name?"

"There's just an initial for the middle name," he said, reviewing his notes.

"It's C, right?"

"It is," Detective Williams said with an open-mouth stare.

"Do you have the name of Charlotte's first husband?" I said, rubbing my head harder.

"I do," he said, maintaining his stare.

"It was George, wasn't it?" I said. "George Smith, right?"

Detective Williams held his notebook up to the light.

"Can you somehow see through this?" he said, stunned. "How the hell did you do that?"

"Clarissa George," I whispered.

"Wow," the Chief said, shaking his head. "Is it possible?"

"You're telling me Clarissa is Charlotte's daughter?" Josie said.

"Yeah, I think I am."

"Holy crap," Detective Williams said. "If you're about to go where I think you are, they were playing a very long game."

"The best grifters always do," I said, then scowled. "Hang on. The prints on the wine glass. They should have been able to match Clarissa's to Prudence."

"There were no prints on Clarissa's glass," Detective Williams said.

"She wiped her glass clean?" Josie said. "Who does that?"

"Force of habit, maybe," Detective Williams said. "She's probably gotten good at covering her tracks."

"Her mother disowns her, and Clarissa decides at some point to either try to reconcile with her or come up with a way to somehow con a bunch of money out of her," I said.

"I gotta ask, Suzy," Josie said. "Because if I don't, it's just going to keep me up at night. How did you tie that together?"

"The counterfeit art scam," I said. "Charlotte is some sort of consultant to the art world." I looked at Detective Williams. "The counterfeiting ring was operating out of New York, wasn't it?"

"It was. But if Clarissa is working with her mother, she must have been looking to reconcile instead of trying to screw her over."

"Maybe," I said. "And it was pretty clear from Charlotte's reaction to the will, she's having some financial trouble."

"They figure out a way to get Clarissa hired by Peters, then they're somehow able to convince Lamplighter's assistant to change the will?" the Chief said.

"That would have been Clarissa's job," I said. "Althea never had a lot of friends."

"What does that have to do with the price of fish?" Josie said.

"She'd be susceptible to someone around her age being friendly to her," Detective Williams said.

"Exactly," I said, nodding.

"Did any of you ever see Clarissa around the area?" the detective said, glancing around the table.

We all shook our heads then I had a thought.

"But Althea liked to come here for drinks after work," I said. "Maybe Millie will remember Clarissa."

"We can arrange that," Detective Williams said.

"Let's start with a photo," I said. "Clarissa was on edge at the lodge the other night. We don't want to do anything that might cause her to run."

"There's just one problem," the Chief said. "Charlotte and Clarissa are pretty small women. Do you think either one of them could have done that much damage to the back of Peters' head? Freddie is convinced he was only hit once."

"If someone was in a rage, I think it's possible," I said.

"P-Squared?" Detective Williams said.

"Sure," the Chief said, nodding. "The estranged brother agreeing to do it for a nice cut of the will. I don't have any problem making that work."

"Maybe," I said, doing my best to rub away the headache that was now dominating my frontal lobe.

Chapter 24

I glanced out the window of my office and watched the dogs as they roamed the play area or napped in the sun. We'd hit the time of year when the snow was gone, but the ground was still partially frozen. As such, we could leave the dogs outside most of the day and not have to worry about the arrival of the spring mud for at least another week. After that we'd begin, weather permitting, a daily bathing ritual that required the entire staff's participation; a ritual that ran between four and six weeks until the sun finally managed to dry the two-acre area out.

I sat down at my desk and reviewed the stack of paperwork needing my attention. I paid bills, reviewed the status of our inventory, then called our accountant to make sure she had everything she needed to process our payroll. Satisfied I was on top of everything, I checked my phone to make sure I hadn't missed any calls then rocked back and forth in my chair, deep in thought.

Josie entered wearing her scrubs and immediately stretched out on the couch. I grabbed a bag of bite-sized from a drawer and tossed it to her.

"Thanks," she said, grabbing a small handful. "Where are the bruisers?"

"I put them out to get some sun," I said, catching the bag when she tossed it back.

"Good call. They can use the exercise. How's Tiny doing today?"

"He's doing great," I said, swiveling around in my chair to take another look out the window. I spotted the Great Dane rolling around on the ground with Chloe.

"That Adequan seems to be working miracles," she said.

"Have you finished all the injections?"

"I've got one more round to go. Tiny hates getting his shots, but we can't argue with the results. His hips are doing much better. With any luck, we've bought him another year or two."

"Well done. My little miracle worker."

"What are you working on?" she said, polishing off the last bite-sized.

"Paying bills. Oh, I just spoke with Marjorie. We actually turned a profit last month."

"Really? We never make money in February. How much?"

"Thirty-seven dollars," I said, laughing.

"Great. Now I can buy that new car," she said, laughing along before turning serious. "What are we going to do with those hybrids?"

"I don't know," I said, shaking my head. "But we've bought ourselves a month."

"Well, the first thing we're going to do as soon as we get the chance is to spay and neuter all of them. Whatever lineage Peters was trying to create stops with that litter of pups."

"Absolutely. But we've got some time. As long as they're caged, we're fine."

"You ever feel like a hypocrite?" Josie said, sitting up. "Because we have several dozen dogs locked up?"

"Yeah."

"No, I don't. Do you?"

"Not really," she said. "But this situation has got me thinking. We keep all the dogs locked up, but our goal with the hybrids is to figure out a way to let them run wild. I know the situation is different, but still."

"There's a huge difference," I said. "Our dogs are social creatures and need to be protected until we can find the right home for them. And they have a pretty good life here."

"Are you kidding? They have a great life."

"And if it were possible for the hybrids to live here, we'd be the first ones to make it happen."

"I know," she said. "But I can't escape the thought we're basically doing the same thing Peters was."

"Some sort of four-legged, social engineering?" I said.

"Yeah, something like that," she said.

"It's not like we're messing around with their genetic makeup. We're just trying to figure out a way the hybrids can live a normal life without being a threat to anyone."

"You're right," Josie said. "But this whole situation is such a…"

"Mess?"

"There's no need to get technical," she said, then stretched back out on the couch. "Yeah, mess is definitely the word for it."

We both glanced at the door when we heard the knock.

"Come on in," I said.

Chief Abrams and Detective Williams entered and looked around.

"Hard at work, huh?" the Chief said, sitting down across from me.

"We're just trying to sort a few things out," I said. "How are you doing, Detective Williams?"

"I'm doing the same thing," he said, sitting down next to the Chief.

"Any luck?" Josie said, sitting up.

"Well, we haven't found anything to disprove our theories," he said. "But we haven't found any proof we're right, either."

"I hate when that happens," Josie said. "How much longer can you make them stick around the area?"

"Not much longer," Detective Williams said. "We need something to provoke a reaction. But we don't have a clue what we could use."

"I'd hate it if we couldn't close this one," the Chief said. "I can't stand the thought of people getting away with murder."

My phone buzzed, and I checked the number. I put the phone on speaker and answered on the second ring.

"Hello, Gerald."

"Hi, Suzy. What's the news on the baby front?"

"Still waiting," I said, gently rubbing my stomach. "You got some news for us?"

"Us?"

"I'm here with Josie and Chief Abrams and Detective Williams."

"Hi, folks," Gerald said. "Well, I don't know if I have anything useful, but I do have some company names Charles Howard is involved with."

"It's a start," I said, reaching for a notepad.

"The guy is very good at covering his tracks," Gerald said. "I'm sure my folks will be able to find more, but they're going to need some time to do any real digging."

"Maybe one of the names will give us something to work with," I said, then glanced at the two cops who nodded in agreement.

"Sure. You ready?"

"Go for it," I said.

"Okay, but there's a bunch of them. Consolidated Imperial, High Tech Limited," Gerald said, pronouncing each name slowly. "General Technologies Incorporated, Twenty-Twenty Enterprises, Global Systems and Strategies."

"Hang on," I said, my neurons flaring. "Go back a couple and say it again."

"Which one?"

"Twenty-something or other."

"Twenty-Twenty Enterprises?" Gerald said.

"That's the one," I said. "What kind of company is it?"

"There's only a general description at this point," Gerald said. "Let's see, Twenty-Twenty Enterprises is some sort of scientific research outfit."

"How about that?" I said, jotting the information down.

"Does that help?" Gerald said.

"It might," I said. "But go ahead and read the rest of the names."

He did and I, along with the Chief and Detective Williams, scribbled the names down. When Gerald finished, I tossed my pen aside.

"That's all I've got for now," Gerald said.

"Thanks, Gerald. We appreciate it."

"You want my guys to keep digging?"

"Yes, please."

"Okay, I'll give you a call as soon as we know more," Gerald said. "And don't forget to remind your mother to call me as soon as the baby is born."

"Will do," I said.

"I need to run. Good luck."

He ended the call, and I put my phone away. Then I noticed the looks all three of them were giving me.

"What?"

"Are you going to tell us?" the Chief said. "Or are we going to have to play twenty-twenty questions?"

"Good one, Chief," I said, laughing. "You remember when I found Peters' password to his computer?"

"I do," the Chief said.

"The password was Project Org 2020," I said. "That can't be a coincidence."

"I'd be surprised if it was," Detective Williams said. "But what's the connection?"

"I don't know," I said with a shrug. "2020 might indicate the year."

"That makes sense," Detective Williams said. "Maybe whatever project the name is referring to is supposed to be completed in 2020."

"Or it's the year the project is supposed to start bearing fruit," I said. "If it's some sort of scientific research project, it probably takes years to come together, right?"

"It's certainly possible," the Chief said. "But what the heck does org stand for?"

"Organization, maybe," Josie said. "It makes sense it would be a part of the company name."

"Organic?" Detective Williams said. "Organize?"

I sat quietly listening to their suggestions, then my neurons flared, and I bolted upright in my chair.

"Holy crap," I whispered as I reached for my laptop and entered a few keywords. A few seconds later, the results of my search came back. I scanned the first page. "That's it."

"Here we go," Josie said, getting off the couch to look over my shoulder. "Holy crap."

"I couldn't have said it better myself," I said, grinning over my shoulder at her.

"What have you got?" Detective Williams said, leaning forward.

"The org stands for organ," I said, turning the screen toward the two cops. "Peters was working on growing human organs in a lab."

"That's impossible," the Chief said.

"Take a look at some of the titles of the recent research studies," I said. "A lot of people have been trying to do it for quite a while."

"And there's been some breakthroughs," Detective Williams said. "Geez, I think you're onto something."

"But who's doing what and why would they kill Peters?" the Chief said. "If he was working on something like this, it has to be worth billions. Peters had to be their golden goose, right?"

"Maybe he was at the point where they didn't need him anymore," Josie said.

"Or Peters was getting cold feet about what he was doing," I said. "Maybe he finally developed some sort of conscience."

"Growing human organs in a lab?" the Chief said. "How is that even possible?"

"Hey, they cloned a sheep back in the nineties," Josie said. "And look at the breakthroughs in DNA research."

"And Peters being the eccentric he was, probably loved the idea of figuring something out nobody believed was possible."

"So, his work with the hybrids was just some sort of cover?" Josie said.

"Maybe. Or just a hobby," I said.

"A hobby?" the Chief said. "Remind me never to make fun of Freddie's origami again."

"I guess my question is, does this make Charles Howard more or less of a suspect?" Detective Williams said.

"That's a good question," I said, nodding at him.

"Thanks. I have my moments," he said, then laughed. "What do you think?"

"I don't know," I said, rubbing my forehead. "I guess it depends on what Peters was up to. If he had a recent breakthrough, you wouldn't think his primary investor would kill him off."

"But if Howard found out Peters was holding out on him, or trying to cut another deal behind his back, I can make it work," the Chief said.

"What about Charlotte?" Detective Williams said. "Maybe all the work she did to invalidate the will was actually related to getting controlling interest in Peters' research."

"I can make that work, too," the Chief said, frowning.

"Me too," Detective Williams said.

"Clarissa," I whispered.

"What about her?" the detective said.

"Whatever the motive was to kill him off, my gut tells me she's somehow in the middle of it," I said.

"You think she could be playing one side off against the other?" Detective Williams said.

"Either that or she's figured out a way to get a cut regardless of what happens," I said.

Chief Abrams and Detective Williams gave it some thought then stared at each other.

"What do you think?" Detective Williams said.

"It's a tough nut to crack," the Chief said. "It would be a lot easier to figure out if Lamplighter's assistant wasn't dead."

I let the Chief's comment roll around in my head, then I leaned forward with my elbows on the desk.

"What if she weren't?"

"What?" Josie said.

"What if she wasn't dead?" I said over my shoulder.

"Suzy, please tell me you're not thinking of trying to recreate her in a lab?" Josie said.

"Funny," I said, then looked at Detective Williams. "Have you told any of the beneficiaries Althea was dead?"

"No, I thought I'd hold that nugget back just in case we needed it," he said.

"Well played," I said, beaming at him. "We need to figure out a way to get the word out that Althea is back in town."

"Doing what?" the Chief said.

"Convalescing, of course," I said.

"In the hospital?" the Chief said.

"No," I said, shaking my head. "At Larry the Loser's house."

Chapter 25

My phone buzzed just before six, and I checked the number and answered immediately.

"Hey, Millie. How's it going?"

"It's deader than the dark of winter here," she said in a controlled whisper. "But guess who just showed up."

"Really?" I said, perking up. "Who's she with?"

"She's by herself," Millie said. "And she's here for dinner."

"Great," I said. "Since you're whispering, I assume she's sitting at the bar."

"She is."

"Do you recognize her?"

"The woman Althea was with had red hair and wore glasses," Millie said. "I guess she could be the same woman, but I'm just not sure."

"Don't worry about it," I said. "We'll be there in five. Keep a couple of seats at the bar open."

"That won't be a problem," she said with a laugh then ended the call.

Josie was already pulling on her coat, and she held the door open for me as we left the office and headed for the registration area. Jill was sitting in front of the computer, and she glanced up when she heard us approach.

"What are you still doing here?" Josie said. "Go home."

"I will in a minute," she said. "I'm just finishing up tomorrow's schedule. Where are you guys off to?"

"The restaurant," I said.

"Maybe we'll see you there later," Jill said. "Sammy and I are celebrating the anniversary of our first date."

"Nice," I said. "The wine's on us."

"Thanks, Suzy."

We left with a wave and headed for my SUV. I opened the door and waited for Josie to give me a hand getting into the passenger seat. She stifled a snort as I climbed in then shut the door behind me. She hopped into the driver seat and glanced over.

"Not a word," I said, glaring at her.

"Wouldn't think of it," she said as she started the engine. "You were quite graceful. All things considered."

"Just drive."

A few minutes later, we parked in the lot behind the restaurant. Determined to do it on my own, I slowly worked my legs out of the car onto solid ground then exhaled loudly.

"Man, this kid better hurry up," I said, then started a slow lumber toward the back door.

We found Chef Claire standing in front of the salad prep area. Several old cookbooks were open and lined up in a long row. She was studying them intensely.

"Hey," she said, glancing up. "I didn't think you guys were coming in tonight."

"Clarissa's here," I said, removing my coat and hanging it on a hook. "What are you doing?"

"Just reviewing some old recipes I might be able to use for retro night."

"What's tonight's special?" Josie said.

"It's seafood gumbo. And for the fish-phobic among us, I made a smaller batch with sausage and chicken."

"Thank you, Chef Claire," I said.

"You should eat more fish," Josie said, heading for the door that led to the dining room. "It's good for you."

"So's yoga," I said, gently punching her on the shoulder. "What's your point?"

We entered the empty lounge, gave Millie a hug, then sat down on either side of Clarissa who was making short work of what looked like scotch on the rocks.

"Hi, Clarissa," I said, slowly working my way onto the stool.

"Hey," she said, glancing back and forth at us. "I was beginning to think I was going to be the only one here tonight."

"It's March," I said with a shrug.

"I can't believe you guys stay open year-round. You must lose your shirts in the winter."

"Yeah," I said. "But people like it."

"I can tell," she deadpanned as she glanced around the empty room.

"Everybody's a comedian," I said. "Are you here by yourself?"

"I am."

"Then you should join us for dinner," I said.

"Yeah, that would be great," Clarissa said.

Millie arrived with a fresh drink for her and a glass of wine for Josie. She placed a club soda with lime in front of me, and I took a long sip.

"Have the cops given you the okay to leave the area?" I said.

"They did. I'm free to go," Clarissa said.

"It'll be nice to get your life back to normal, huh?" Josie said.

"It certainly will," Clarissa said, then turned to me. "When's your due date?"

"A week from tomorrow," I said, rubbing my belly.

"Do you know what you're having?"

"A girl."

"Good for you," Clarissa said, tossing back what was left of her drink and pushing the empty glass forward. She began stirring the fresh one. "Let's hope you have a better relationship with your daughter than my mom did with me."

"I'm sorry to hear that," I said. "You want to talk about it?"

"No, I do not," she said, then took a long sip.

"Got it."

"Did you get a chance to call Larry?" Josie said, leaning in front of Clarissa.

"I did," I said. "He can make it. He said she'll be fine by herself for a few hours."

"Good," Josie said. "I imagine he can use a break."

Clarissa, her interest piqued, glanced back and forth at us.

"Larry?"

"Yeah, Larry Lamplighter," I said.

"The lawyer who screwed up Jeremy's will?"

"The one and only," I said, then chuckled. "It's going to take him forever to live that one down."

"We can only hope," Clarissa said. "So, what are you doing with him?"

"We invited him to family dinner tomorrow," I said. "We do it one night a week."

"That sounds like fun. My mother's idea of a family dinner was us going through the drive-thru in the same car," Clarissa said, then frowned. "You mentioned he needed a break. From what?"

"He's been taking care of someone who had an accident," Josie said, casually tossing it out.

"What sort of accident?"

"Car crash," I said. "His former assistant went off the side of a mountain in Colorado."

Clarissa flinched and glanced back and forth at us as if her head were on a swivel.

"She went off a mountain and lived?"

"Yeah, apparently the doctors said it was a miracle," Josie said. "Her car landed in a bunch of pine trees that somehow managed to break her fall. Well, at least enough for her to survive the crash."

"Wow," Clarissa whispered.

"She was very lucky," I said.

"She certainly was," Clarissa said, staring straight ahead into the mirror behind the bar. "I mean, she had to be, right? Going off a mountain like that. How long has she been out of the hospital?"

"Well, I think Althea got into town a couple of days ago," Josie said. "Larry flew her back as soon as she got released. But she's still pretty banged up. Larry said it's a round-the-clock job taking care of her."

"That's why we decided to invite him to dinner," I said. "You know, so he can relax a bit."

"But she's okay being by herself?" Clarissa said.

"Larry says she'll be fine for a few hours," Josie said, then played the next card perfectly. "What was that thing he was talking about the other day when we ran into him at the store?"

"It didn't make a lot of sense," I said. "He was babbling. Some sort of scientific papers the cops found in Althea's car."

"Scientific papers?" Clarissa said.

"Yeah," I said. "Larry thinks they belonged to Peters. Project something or other. It was way over my head."

"Mine too," Josie said. "I wonder how Althea got her hands on them."

"Maybe Peters gave them to her for safekeeping," I said. "Or she stole them."

"Well, Althea does have a reputation for playing fast and loose with the rules," Josie said.

"I hope she'll be okay at Larry's house by herself," I said.

"If she weren't, he wouldn't have agreed to come to dinner," Josie said.

"What sort of injuries does she have?" Clarissa said, casually stirring her drink.

"Do you remember what Larry said?" Josie said, again leaning forward to make eye contact. "It was a long list."

"Broken leg. Maybe a cracked pelvis?" I said, frowning. "I can't remember all of them."

"Lots of cuts," Josie said. "But the doctors are most worried about the head injury. She's got a nasty concussion."

"Oh," I said, raising a finger. "Don't forget the tongue laceration."

"Yuk," Josie said, making a face at me. "Don't remind me."

"She cut her tongue?" Clarissa said.

"Yeah, it took something like forty stitches to sew it up," I said. "She almost bit it off on impact."

"Suzy," Josie said with a scowl. "Must you? We're about to have dinner."

"Sorry," I said. "Larry said she's still not able to talk."

"Really?" Clarissa said. "But she's able to write stuff down, right? You know, so she can tell people what she needs."

"Not with two broken arms," I said, shaking my head. "So, until she's a bit better, I guess the cops are going to have to wait to hear her side of the story."

"Her side of the story?" Clarissa said, raising an eyebrow at me.

"Yeah. You know, her take on how she managed to drive her car off a cliff," I said.

"Oh, right," Clarissa said, then drained the last of her drink. "I need to wash up before dinner."

"We'll be here," I said, watching her head for the bathroom.

"Well played," Josie said.

"You too," I said. "Ten bucks she bails on dinner."

"I'll take that bet," Josie said. "She's gonna want to pump us for more information."

"Nah. She's got enough."

"What are you two up to?" Millie said.

"We're trying to catch a rat," I said. "Maybe more than one."

Clarissa returned and immediately grabbed her coat from the back of her stool.

"I'm really sorry," she said. "But I'm going to have to pass on dinner. I just remembered I have a conference call scheduled tonight."

"Conference call?" Josie said.

"Yeah, it's with this company I'm doing some work for out on the west coast," Clarissa said. "They're wondering where the heck I've been and are starting to get a little cranky about my absence."

"Sorry to hear that," I said. "But duty calls, right?"

"Exactly."

"Hey, I've got an idea," Josie said. "Why don't you come to family dinner tomorrow night?"

"Tomorrow night?" Clarissa said. "Uh…actually, I was thinking about getting on the road in the afternoon."

"Maybe you can fit dinner in before you go," I said. "You gotta eat, right?"

"I'll see what I can do," she said, zipping her coat. "If I can make it, what time I should be there?"

"Seven," I said. "And you'll be out of there by nine, nine-thirty at the latest."

"Okay. Thanks. I'll do my best."

"I'm sure you will," I said, extending my hand. "Nice seeing you, Clarissa."

"Yeah, you too," she said, returning the handshake. "Later."

We watched her depart then I motioned at Josie with my hand. She dug into her pocket and slid a ten-dollar bill down the bar.

"Thanks for playing," I said, pocketing the ten.

"Lucky guess," she said, then sat back as Millie topped her wine glass off. "Let's eat."

"Remind me to call the Chief after dinner."

"Will do," she said, hopping off her stool. "And we also need to call Larry."

"Yeah. It's probably not a good idea for him to be home tomorrow night."

Chapter 26

Josie parked the van on the same dead-end street we'd used the day Peters' will was read and turned the engine off. I glanced over my shoulder and couldn't miss the befuddled look on Larry the Loser's face.

"Tell me again why I'm doing surveillance on my own house."

"Because you'll be useful as an eyewitness," I said.

"Says who?" he said.

"Judge Thompson," I said.

"Thompson? That guy hates my guts," the lawyer said, his voice rising.

"That's beside the point at the moment, Larry," I said, then pointed at the duffel bag next to him on the back seat. "Hand me that bag, please."

Josie took it from him and held it while I rummaged around. I removed the laser microphone from the bag and attached it to the passenger side mirror. Then I grabbed three earpieces from the bag and passed them out. I inserted mine then fiddled with the wireless device that controlled the microphone.

"Can you guys hear me?" I said into a walkie-talkie.

"Loud and clear," the Chief said. "Remember we're going to be turning our radios off as soon as somebody shows up. From that point, you won't be able to talk to us."

"Got it," I said. "But all that matters is what we hear going on inside the house."

"Don't forget to press the record button," the Chief said.

"Hey, do I look an amateur?" I said. "Where are you guys?"

"We're hiding in the coat room outside Larry's office," Detective Williams said.

"Kind of a tight fit, isn't it?" Larry said.

"Yeah," the Chief said. "I can think of better ways to spend the evening. No offense, Detective Williams."

"None taken. And for the record, you're no dream date yourself."

"Did Judge Thompson give you any problems today?" I said.

"No," Detective Williams said. "He said as long as Larry didn't have a problem with it, he'd sign off."

"How disappointed was he when you told him I wasn't involved?" Larry said.

"Maybe a little," Detective Williams said. "But I think he was more surprised than anything."

"Not that it's going to matter," Larry said. "By the time Peters' widow gets through with me, I'll be a footnote."

"Maybe not," I said, then spotted a solitary figure casually strolling down the street. "Here we go. A woman on foot is heading our way."

"Who is it?" the Chief said.

"Hang on," I said, reaching for my binoculars. "It's Charlotte." I held out my hand. "Told you she'd be the first one here."

"Dang it," Josie said, digging a ten out of her pocket and handing it over.

"Did you remember to leave the front door unlocked?" I said to Larry.

"I did. I hardly ever lock it."

"You might want to start," Josie said, glancing into the backseat.

We watched Charlotte head up the front steps. She paused on the porch, glanced around, then opened the door.

"Okay, radios off," Detective Williams said.

"Have fun," I said, then turned the walkie-talkie off and tossed it into the duffel bag.

We sat quietly then the lights in the front room came on.

"Pretty brave to turn the lights on like that," Josie said.

"It's better than having somebody see a flashlight beam coming from the house," I said.

"Fair point," Josie said, nodding.

We listened to the sound of drawers being opened and closed, then a thought popped.

"Uh-oh," I said.

"What?" Josie said.

"I'm just wondering what's going to happen if Charlotte decides to look in the coat room."

"You're just thinking of that now?" Josie said.

"Hey, I didn't tell them to hide there."

"Well, if she does, they'll have some serious 'splainin' to do, huh?"

"Two cops with a legitimate warrant," I said, shrugging. "They should be fine."

"Here he comes," Larry said, pointing out the window.

"Right on time," I said. "I can't wait to hear what Charles and Charlotte have to say to each other."

We watched as Charles Howard climbed the steps two at a time. He paused when he noticed the lights were on but eventually slowly opened the front door and disappeared from sight. A few seconds later, both their voices could be heard loud and clear.

"What are you doing here?" Charlotte said.

"I was about to ask you the same thing," Charles Howard said.

"I'm here for a meeting with the lawyer," Charlotte said. "I called him earlier and told him I wanted to see if there's a way we could work all this out without having to go to court."

"That's a lie," Larry said from the backseat. "She never did any such thing."

"You don't say," Josie deadpanned with a roll of her eyes.

"Oh, right," Larry said. "It's her cover story. Never mind."

"Why don't I believe you, Charlotte?" Charles said.

"I really don't care if you believe me or not," she said. "What's your excuse?"

"He called and said he had a document that looked like it belonged to me."

"Right," Charlotte said with a snort. "Nice try."

"Man, these people lie more than I do," Larry said.

"And that's not easy, huh?" I said.

"You got that right," Larry said.

"Shhh," Josie said.

"What sort of document are you talking about?" Charlotte said.

"It was just some stuff related to his wolf research," Charles said, going for casual.

I spotted Clarissa walking briskly down the street and heading straight for the house.

"There she is."

"I can't wait to find out which one she's working with," Josie said.

"She's working with both of them," I said.

"What?" Josie said, glancing over at me.

"Yeah," I said, nodding. "But I don't think either one of them knows she's working both sides of the street."

"You want to go double or nothing on that?"

"I wouldn't if I were you," I said with a grin. "Now hush."

We watched Clarissa enter the house. I turned the volume of our earpieces up a notch.

"What are you doing here?" Charles Howard said. "You said you had a dinner invitation."

"I did," Clarissa said. "But I didn't say I was going."

"Dinner with who?" Charlotte said.

"That idiot lawyer and the dog muttonheads."

"Muttonhead?" Larry said from the backseat.

"Idiot. Nitwit," Josie said over her shoulder.

"Harsh," I said, laughing.

"Yeah," Josie said. "What did we ever do to her?"

"You mean, apart from ruining her plans, right?"

"There is that," Josie said.

"I was just asking him what he's doing here," Charlotte said. "He said he's here to collect some of Jeremy's wolf research. I don't believe a word of it."

"That's not why he's here," Clarissa said.

"You know why he's here?" Charlotte said.

"Of course, I do. He's here because I invited him."

"What's that?" Charlotte said, obviously on edge.

"Most people would call it a gun," Clarissa said. "But just for the sake of clarity, this is a Beretta M9A3 with a silencer. Nice, huh?"

"What are you doing with a gun?" Charlotte said.

"Well, I need it to finish the job your so-called expert screwed up in Colorado," Clarissa said. "Stay here. I'll be right back."

We heard the sound of footsteps.

"She's heading upstairs to look for Althea," I said.

"But Althea's dead," Larry said.

"Yes, we know that, Larry," I said. "But they don't."

"Got it."

Moments later, we heard another round of footsteps.

"She's not here," Clarissa said.

"Who's not here?" Charles said.

"Althea. The lawyer's assistant."

"The one who went off a cliff?" Charles said.

"How did you know that?" Clarissa said.

"The cops mentioned it today when they were grilling me," Charles said casually.

"He's good," I said.

"Imagine my surprise when I heard she was still alive," Clarissa said. "How the heck did he manage to screw that up?"

"I have no idea," Charlotte said. "But I'm certainly going to find out."

"*Oh, don't worry. I've got it covered,*" Clarissa said in a mocking tone. "What is he again? A ski instructor who moonlights as a hit man?"

"He told me it was taken care of," Charlotte said. "She's really not here?"

"Did you hear a loud pop?" Clarissa snapped. "The muttonheads said she was in bad shape. She must have relapsed. But, no worries. As soon as I finish up here, I'll swing by the hospital and take care of it."

"I'm missing something here," Charles Howard said. "You tried to kill that woman?"

"Well, we really couldn't have her walking around running her mouth," Clarissa said. "But it turns out the idiot you hired couldn't handle one simple thing. I guess the old saying is true. If you want something done right, do it yourself."

"Don't speak to me in that tone, Prudence," Charlotte said.

"How many times do I have to tell you, *Mother*? My name is Clarissa."

"There's no need to be cruel. Whatever problems we've had over the years, I'm still your mother."

"Don't remind me."

"Uh, can we back up a bit?" Charles Howard said. "She's your mother?"

"Surprised, huh?" Clarissa said with an evil laugh that made the hairs on the back of my neck stand up.

"So, you working with Jeremy was part of some elaborate setup you two came up with?" Charles Howard said.

"*I* came up with it," Clarissa said. "She was just along for the ride. And she couldn't even handle one simple thing."

"You're not going to let it go, are you?" Charlotte said, playing defense. "And I handled everything else perfectly."

"I guess that remains to be seen," Clarissa said. "Let's continue this conversation in the office. It has to be in there."

"What are you talking about?" Charlotte said.

"I'm talking about the reason I'm standing here dealing with you two," Clarissa said. "Sit down on that couch."

We listened to the sound of desk drawers being opened and closed then heard the loud thump of something landing on what I assumed was the desk.

"What's that?" Charlotte said.

"He had it in his office the whole time?" Charles said, obviously stunned.

"No, according to the muttonheads, the cops found it in Althea's car," Clarissa said.

"Muttonhead," Josie said, glancing over at me. "I don't think I like it."

"Me either," I said. "It has a rather pejorative tone."

"I know that one," Larry said, leaning forward. "Derogatory, right?"

We both glanced over our shoulders and stared at him.

"Never mind," he said, sitting back.

"What is that?" Charlotte said.

"I just told you, *Mother*. It's the reason we're here."

"There's eight-million dollars in that envelope?"

"Geez," Clarissa grunted, the contempt in her voice unmistakable. "You're such an idiot. Are they putting something in the water supply down there?"

"Well, I'm sorry I'm not able to keep track of all the scams you're working on," Charlotte said. "You should have seen the time she stole all my credits cards and maxed them out on Pokemon cards."

"It was a better investment than anything you've ever come up with," Clarissa said.

"Pokemon cards?" Charles said.

"I was eight," Clarissa snapped.

"Right after that was her first trip to juvenile hall," Charlotte said.

"Yeah," Clarissa said. "I went in a babe in the woods and came out with a whole bunch of new ideas."

"And you tried them all," Charlotte said. "Look Pru-, Clarissa, I love sitting here reminiscing about your delightful childhood, but I thought you dragged me over here for another reason."

"You hear that?" Clarissa said.

"Hear what?" Charles Howard said.

"The condescending tone in her voice," Clarissa said. "You never change, do you, *Mother*?"

"This is ridiculous," Charlotte said. "Can we get to it? You said you'd found a handwritten copy of the original will."

"I lied," Clarissa said. "There is a handwritten copy around somewhere. But Jeremy must have stashed it away. Either that or the cops have it. And since they might, we need to wrap this up. I need to hit the road."

"Where are you going?" Charlotte said.

"That is none of your business. Not that it's going to matter. Who are you going to tell?"

"I guess that depends," Charlotte said. "Assuming I need to, I'll talk to whoever can help me."

"Uh, Charlotte," Charles said. "I don't think that's what she's referring to."

"I'm not following," Charlotte said.

"A half-step behind as always," Clarissa said, laughing.

"What on earth are you talking about?"

"She's going to kill us, Charlotte."

"What?"

"Well done, Charles," Clarissa said. "Now I understand why you've risen to the top of your field."

"Why would she kill us?" Charlotte said. "After she told me she had figured out a way to get around Jeremy's will, I promised her two million from the estate."

"Two million, huh?" Charles said, then chuckled.

"What's wrong with two million?"

"Do the math, Charlotte," Charles said. "Last time I looked, eight is a lot more than two."

"You wouldn't dare," Charlotte said, her voice rising. "You want to spend the rest of your life on the run?"

"Why would I be running? I'm going to be the grief-stricken daughter who was shocked to hear her mother and her dead husband's investor were both killed in a tragic murder-suicide. Maybe the cops will think the two of you had some sort of lover's tiff. That would certainly juice the story."

"What?"

"C'mon, *Mother*. Make an effort to use what's left of your brain. At least try to follow along."

"Even if I can understand why you might want to kill me, what on earth has Charles done to you?"

"Nothing, really," Clarissa said. "Let's just say Charles is collateral damage."

"Because he killed Jeremy?" Charlotte said.

"Wow," Charles said, baffled. "When she said you were a little dense, she wasn't joking."

"I told ya," Clarissa said.

"You didn't kill Jeremy?" Charlotte said.

"Why would I do that?" Charles said. "He was on the verge of making both of us a whole lot of money."

"Which Jeremy wasn't willing to share," Clarissa said.

"Then who killed him?" Charlotte said.

"Really?" Charles said. "You really need to ask that question?"

We waited out an extended silence, then Charlotte whispered.

"You killed him?"

"Wow," Charles said again.

"I feel like I'm in a Fellini movie," Clarissa said. "Yes, *Mother*. I killed Jeremy."

"But we were going to wait and let my guy in Colorado handle that," Charlotte said.

"I couldn't take the chance of waiting," Clarissa said. "He was getting too close."

"Too close to what?" Charlotte said, her voice rising again.

"To that," Charles said.

"What is it?" Charlotte said.

"Well, unless I'm mistaken, that envelope contains the latest results of Jeremy's research," Charles said.

"His work with the wolves?" Charlotte said, increasingly confused.

"Geez, Mother. You were married to the guy. How could you not know what he was working on?"

"I never paid much attention to his work," Charlotte said. "And who could even begin to understand all that crap?"

"Inside this envelope is information that's potentially worth billions," Clarissa said.

"Billions?" Charlotte said. "Is she telling the truth?"

"She is," Charles said, then paused before continuing. "You really thought I killed him?"

"I did. I figured you wanted your investment money back and had finally run out of patience."

Clarissa snorted loudly.

"Did I say something funny?" Charlotte snapped.

"Want his money back? He was about to drop a hundred million into Jeremy's lap," Clarissa said.

"A hundred million? On wolf research?"

"No. On the prospect of growing human organs in a laboratory," Clarissa said. "And I wasn't going to see any of it."

"But how is that possible?" Charlotte said.

"Who knows? That's why I needed the envelope," Clarissa said. "But the guy was a genius."

"He certainly was," Charles said. "A total wingnut, but definitely a genius."

"But how did you end up being part of this?" Charlotte said.

"I was about to ask the same question," Josie whispered.

"Shhh," I said, listening closely.

"Clarissa called me out of the blue," Charles said. "Told me Jeremy was getting cold feet about his research. She said he was ranting and raving about how he was going to go to hell for messing around with God's work."

"And you believed her?" Charlotte said.

"Hey, if there's one thing I learned over the years, when it came to Jeremy's behavior, anything was possible."

"I can't argue with that," Charlotte said. "So, she agreed to hand over Jeremy's research before he did something crazy?"

"She told me he was threatening to burn it," Charles said.

"I thought that was a nice touch," Clarissa said. "And it certainly got your attention."

"Yeah, it sure did," Charles said.

"How much did you offer her?" Charlotte said.

"Ten million," Charles said. "But at some point, she must have decided she could get a lot more. Especially if I was out of the picture. What's the plan, Clarissa? You going to show up at the next board meeting with that envelope?"

"No, I'm going with a one on one approach," Clarissa said. "From what I understand, your second in charge has been dying to take over for years. This oughta do the trick, huh?"

"You've done your homework," Charles said.

"Thanks," Clarissa said. "For what it's worth, Charles, I'm sorry I have to take you out."

"Yeah. I can tell you're heartbroken."

"Maybe they'll put your name in lights on the new lab. Or name a kidney after you."

"When you called me and said you had come up with a way to get our hands on Jeremy's money, I thought we had finally turned the corner."

"No, *Mother*," Clarissa said. "We weren't turning the corner. It's just one more dead end."

"I can't believe you're going to kill us," Charlotte whispered.

"Actually, the way it's going to look is that you killed Charles, then killed yourself," Clarissa said. "Right here in the shyster's office."

"Can I ask you a favor?" Charles said.

"A favor? Interesting," Clarissa said. "Sure, why not? What do you need?"

"I'd love to see what's in that envelope before I go," Charles said.

"I suppose we can do that," Clarissa said.

"Here we go," I whispered.

"What?" Josie said, glancing over.

"She's going to have to put the gun down to open the envelope," I said.

"That's why you wanted the duct tape, right?"

"Yup."

"Geez," Clarissa said. "Whatever is in this thing must be good. Fort Knox would be easier to get into."

We heard the sound of metal on wood, then Clarissa emitted a round of grunts as she struggled to get the envelope open.

"Now," I whispered.

"What?" Josie said.

We heard the sound of a door opening followed by Charlotte's scream.

"Hands in the air," Detective Williams shouted.

"Don't even think about it, Clarissa," Chief Abrams said. "I'd much rather see you in orange than on the slab."

"On the slab?" Josie said.

"Yeah, a bit hackneyed," I said. "He's better than that."

"Charles, if you'd be so kind," Detective Williams said. "Put these handcuffs on Charlotte."

"In front or back?"

"Front is fine," the detective said. "I don't think she's going to give us any trouble. Are you, Charlotte?"

"I'm merely here for a meeting with my lawyer," she said softly.

But her heart wasn't in it, and we heard the sound of two sets of handcuffs being snapped on.

"Why aren't you putting him in cuffs?" Clarissa said.

"Because he didn't do anything," Detective Williams said.

"He offered me ten million bucks for that envelope," Clarissa said.

"From what I heard, he was merely paying for something he already owned," the Chief said. "I imagine he considered it a business expense. Isn't that right, Charles?"

"That's certainly the way I was going to play it," he said. "And thanks for the call. Without it, I might have walked into something I couldn't get out of."

"No problem," Detective Williams said. "I just wish it had been my idea."

"The Muttonheads," Clarissa said, almost spitting the words out. "It was them, wasn't it?"

"Maybe," the Chief said. "Okay, folks. You can come in whenever you're ready."

"I thought he'd never ask," I said, opening my door.

Josie came around to my side of the van and helped me out. Then the three of us made our way into the house. We walked down the hall and entered the office. Clarissa and Charlotte were on the couch. Charlotte continued to glance around the office with a deer in the headlights look seemingly etched in place. Clarissa glared at me, then did the same to Josie and Larry.

"Muttonheads?" Josie said, returning her stare.

"It seemed to fit," Clarissa said. "Althea's dead, isn't she?"

"She is," I said, nodding. "Ski instructor, huh, Charlotte?"

"If I give you his name, can I cut some sort of deal?" she said, glancing back and forth at the cops.

"I don't like your chances," Detective Williams said.

"You mind answering a couple of questions?" I said to Clarissa.

"I guess we'll see," she said, maintaining her glare.

"This all started when Peters asked you to witness the handwritten will, right?"

Clarissa gave it some thought, then nodded.

"He wrote it down in his office," I said. "At the place where he was doing his real research."

"Yeah, Charles gave him office and lab space to use at one of his facilities," Clarissa said.

"I did," Charles said.

"And at some point, he decided to move into Cabot Lodge?" I said.

"He'd been going back and forth for several months while the renovations were going on," Clarissa said. "Then he decided to pack up all the hybrids and move in permanently."

"So, you spent time with him at the lodge?" I said.

"No, I just followed him one day," she said.

"Right after he let you know you weren't getting a cut from the next round of funding?"

"Yeah," she said, nodding. "I wasn't very happy about it."

"Now, there's an understatement," Josie said.

"How much did you offer Althea to help you change the will?"

"Enough," she said. "Not that she was ever going to see most of it."

"Because you decided to kill her off, right?"

"That was her decision," Clarissa said, pointing at her mother.

"She's lying," Charlotte said. "It was her idea."

"Nice try, Mother."

"And the book mentioned in the will?" I said. "The Origin of Species."

"What about it?" Clarissa said.

"It wasn't mentioned in the handwritten version you witnessed. You had Althea add it."

"I did."

"Because you weren't named as a beneficiary and needed a way to be invited to the reading of the will?" I said.

"That was definitely part of it," she said. "But I also wanted the book. I'm a collector."

"I knew it," I said, beaming as I glanced around the room. "I knew you had to be a collector."

"Why does that even matter?" Clarissa said, baffled.

306

"It was bugging me," I whispered with a shrug.

"You really are kinda weird, aren't you?"

"Yeah, I should probably start working on that."

"Would anybody mind if I opened this?" Charles said, waving the envelope in the air.

"Knock yourself out," Detective Williams said. "I wouldn't mind seeing it myself."

We waited quietly as Charles used a pair of scissors to cut through my wrapping job. Then he slowly removed a thick document and casually flipped through it. Then he started laughing and didn't stop.

"What is it?" Clarissa said.

"It's a photocopy version of Jack London's *Call of the Wild*," he said, tossing the document on the desk.

"Nice touch," Josie said.

"Thanks. I knew you'd appreciate it."

"So, I guess that means Jeremy hadn't had a breakthrough after all, right?" Charlotte said.

"No," Clarissa said. "It just means he hid his research someplace where nobody can find it."

"It'll turn up," Charles said. "Eventually."

"Okay, Chief," Detective Williams said. "What do you say we get these two started on their new lives?"

We watched as they helped both women to their feet then led them out of the office.

"Nice work," Detective Williams said.

"It was a group effort," I said.

"Yeah, maybe," he said, then departed with a wave over his shoulder.

Josie sat down on the couch and put her feet up on the coffee table. Larry sat down behind his desk and flipped through the document. Then he focused on Charles Howard.

"You going to need any legal help sorting all this out?" Larry said.

"Oh, I'm going to need a bunch," he said, sitting down in a chair across from the lawyer. "But before you ask, I've already got more lawyers than I know what to do with."

"Yeah," Larry said, despondent. "I'm sure you do. Oh, well, it couldn't hurt to ask, right?"

"What do you think is going to happen with Jeremy's estate?" I said.

"I imagine it depends on how hard Charlotte's lawyers want to push it and the judge who catches the case," Charles said.

"A judge will sort all this out?" I said, my neurons surging.

"Since Jeremy is dead, and Charlotte and Clarissa are both going to be in jail, that would be my guess. Why do you ask?"

"We're worried about what's going to happen to the hybrids," I said.

"Well, if you can convince the judge what Jeremy's real intentions were, maybe your friend will be able to keep that hunting lodge. That would help, wouldn't it?"

"It would be a start," I said. "But you're going to want the right to bring a bunch of people out there and go through the place with a fine-toothed comb."

"Yes, I'm afraid I'll have to insist," Charles said.

"You really think Jeremy cracked the code on growing organs?" Josie said.

"I do," Charles said. "It's going to revolutionize science and medicine."

"It's a bit Dr. Frankenstein, wouldn't you say?" Josie said.

"Not if you're someone who's lost a limb or is waiting for a transplant," he said with a shrug.

"They're going to be able to regrow limbs?" Larry said, stunned.

"Probably not at first," Charles said. "But who knows what we'll be able to do in the coming years?"

"I'm not comfortable with any of this," Josie said.

"You're a dog lover, right?"

"Yeah, I guess you could say that," she said, grinning at me.

"Then suppose you had the ability to clone your favorite dog," he said without emotion. "Recreate it completely. A different animal that was identical to the one you had to say goodbye to. Would you do it?"

Josie and I looked at each other as we gave the question some serious thought. Eventually, Josie glanced back at Charles Howard and nodded.

"Yes, I would," she whispered.

"There you go," he said, spreading his hands to emphasize the point. "And if you were a mother whose kid needed new kidneys?"

"I'd do it in a heartbeat," I said, rubbing my stomach.

"Most people would," he said, removing a business card from his wallet. "I need to run. I'll be in touch. But if you have any questions for me, or need anything, don't hesitate to call. And good luck with the baby."

"Thanks," I said, pressing a hand against my stomach.

We watched him depart. Then Josie got to her feet and jangled the keys to the van.

310

"You ready to go?" she said. "I think the kitchen might still be open. I'm starving."

"Yeah, just give me sec," I said, feeling a strange sensation.

"Are you okay?" Josie said.

"Yeah, I think so," I said, then looked at Larry. "Remember how I promised not to *pop* in your office?"

"I do," Larry said. "Please tell me you're not going to do that."

"No, I'm not," I said, staring down at the carpet. "But I probably should tell you my water just broke."

Epilogue

Exhausted, but elated, I glanced down at my daughter who was nestled against my chest, sound asleep. I gently stroked her head and let loose with a contented sigh.

"She's so beautiful," my mother said, unable to take her eyes off the baby. "Maxine Joclaire Chandler. Welcome to the world."

"Little Max," Josie said with a grin. "I can't wait to watch her grow up. I have so much to teach her."

"Like how to eat a chili-dog without spilling it all over yourself?" I said.

"Josie needs to figure out how to do it first," Chef Claire said.

"Do as I say, not as I do?" I said, laughing.

"Exactly," Chef Claire said.

"Shut it."

The baby woke up and kicked her legs as she let loose with a yawn. She stared up at me, and another wave of emotion washed over me.

"Oh, good," my mother said. "She's awake. Can I hold her, darling?"

"Of course, Mom."

My mother gently lifted Max and tucked the blanket around her. Then she rocked the baby and forth in her arms.

"She likes you, Mrs. C.," Chef Claire said.

"She better," Josie said with a laugh. "Grandma just set her up with a trust fund."

"Hush," my mother said, grinning at Josie.

"If I let you cuddle me, will you set one up for me, too?" Josie said.

"You're not that cute," my mother said, then cooed to the baby. "Your Aunt Josie thinks she's so funny, doesn't she?"

Chief Abrams and Detective Williams gently knocked on the open door but remained in the doorway.

"Can we come in?" the Chief said.

"Absolutely," I said, raising the bed. "What's the latest?"

"Well, we're still working up all the charges," Detective Williams said. "It's a long list."

"Did you get a chance to talk to Judge Thompson?"

"We did," Detective Williams said. "Based on the different versions of the will we showed him, he thinks there's a good chance Lacey will be able to keep Cabot Lodge."

"The handwritten version was the clincher," the Chief said. "Judge Thompson says it indicates Peters' *true intent*."

"That's great news. Do you think Charlotte is going to try and fight it?"

"I doubt if Charlotte is going to be worrying about anything other than staying out of jail," the Chief said.

"Is that even a possibility?" I said.

"Highly doubtful," Detective Williams said.

Lacey poked her head through the door and looked around.

"Should I come back later?" she said. "It looks like you're having a party."

"No, come on in," I said. "There's plenty of room."

"Oh, my goodness," Lacey said, getting her first look at the baby. "She's perfect."

"Thanks," I said, beaming.

"She is, isn't she?" my mother said, staring down at her granddaughter.

"Is Rooster here with you?"

"He spent all morning clearing some brush, and now he's working on his truck," Lacey said, shaking her head. "The guy never stops moving. He said to tell you he'll be stopping by the house tomorrow. You are still getting discharged today, right?"

"I am. You guys want to tell her the good news?"

"The judge thinks you'll be able to keep Cabot Lodge," the Chief said.

"Really?"

"Yeah," Detective Williams said. "Congrats. What are you going to do with the place?"

"I imagine I'll live there," she said. "At least most of the year. I'll play the winters by ear. But we need to figure out what we're going to do with the hybrids."

"There is that," Josie said.

"We can't keep them caged up," Lacey said. "That's no life for them."

"No, it's not," I said, then a thought floated to the surface. "Maybe we're looking at it wrong."

"This is the part where we just sit quietly and wait for her to continue, right?" Lacey said.

"You're a quick study," Josie said, laughing. "Okay, Snoopmeister. What have you got?"

I pushed myself further up in the bed to get more comfortable. I smiled as I watched my mom gently rock the baby who'd fallen back asleep.

"The hybrids are becoming a problem all over the place, right?" I said.

"They are," Josie said. "For lots of reasons."

"But what's the biggest problem?" I said.

"It's the same problem we're trying to deal with," Josie said. "What do you do with a wild animal that's partially socialized?"

"Right," I said. "You can't turn them loose, and you can't have them around the house as pets."

"Limbo Land," Josie said, nodding.

"Then instead of trying to figure out what we're going to do with the ones out at the lodge, maybe we should be looking at ways to help as many of the hybrids as we can."

Josie frowned as she thought about my comment, then the penny dropped.

"You're talking about creating a hybrid sanctuary," Josie said.

"I am," I said, grinning at her. Then I focused on Lacey. "Do you remember how many acres Cabot Lodge sits on?"

"A little over five hundred," she said.

"That would be enough," Josie said. "But you'd still have to feed them. They're way too dependent on people by now to make them fend for themselves."

"Yeah," I said, nodding.

"And you'd need to fence it," Lacey said. "Five hundred acres? That's one big fence."

"It is," I said. "But ranchers out west build massive fences all the time. And some of those places are thousands of acres."

"I love the idea," Lacey said. "There's just one problem."

"The cost of the fence," I said.

"You're not planning on paying for it, are you?" Josie said.

"No, I'm certainly not. Mom?"

"Don't look at me, darling," she said, cradling the baby in her arms. "I have other plans for my money these days."

"No, I wasn't asking you to pay for it," I said. "But if we set up the sanctuary as a non-profit, you could shake the trees for donations, couldn't you?"

"I suppose I could make a few calls," she said.

"Thanks. Oh, before I forget. Remember to give Gerald a call and let him know it's okay for him to keep accepting contributions from Charles Howard."

"I'll do that," my mother said, beaming down at the baby and gently stroking her head.

"How did you know Charles wasn't involved in Jeremy's murder?" Lacey said. "You guys took quite a chance letting him know what he was walking into at that lawyer's office.

"Not really," Detective Williams said, shaking his head.

"Two reasons," I said. "The first was the fact that Jeremy's research was actually panning out. And there's no way Charles would do anything to jeopardize it. If he could have figured out a way to do it, he probably would have put Peters in one of those plastic bubbles just to keep him safe."

"I guess that makes sense," Lacey said.

"The second reason was the way Charles reacted all the time. Especially the night we had the dinner party at the hunting lodge. His eyes were constantly moving around. Like he was trying to figure out where Peters could have hidden his research. It was pretty clear that was his only focus. The rest of the stuff with Clarissa and Charlotte was just a sideshow to him."

"A corporate guy who was keeping his eyes on the prize," Detective Williams said.

"But he could've had someone else kill Jeremy," Lacey said.

"Not with that much at stake," I said, shaking my head.

"Yeah, you're probably right," she said. "But it was still a gutsy move tipping him off like that. I would have been worried about being wrong and having it blow up in my face."

"If it had, we were in the coat room with guns," the Chief said.

"Hang on," I said, staring at Lacey. "Say that again."

"What? The part about it blowing up in my face?"

"No, the other thing," I said, rubbing my forehead.

"I said it was a gutsy move to tip him off," Lacey said.

"Gutsy," I said, then focused on Detective Williams. "You wouldn't happen to have Peters' journal with you? You know, the one with all the drawings and rambling passages."

"I do," the detective said. "We had to bring everything with us when we met with Judge Thompson this morning. Why?"

"Dig it out," I said, raising the bed as far as it would go.

He rummaged through his bag then removed the journal from an evidence bag.

"Near the back, one of Peter's last entries, there's a short poem. If I remember, it's a pair of rhyming couplets."

Detective Williams flipped through the pages then came to a stop.

"The one called The Final Reveal?" he said.

"That's it," I said. "Read it out loud."

"Ignore the howls, they're not for you. Ignore bared teeth, it's what they do. Does the money man have the guts? To prove to all, that I'm not nuts."

Detective Williams glanced up from the journal and frowned.

"Robert Frost, he's not," Josie said.

"No," I said. "But it's all there."

"I'm sorry, Suzy," the Chief said. "But I'm going to need a little more."

"Good," Detective Williams said, staring at me. "I'm glad to hear I'm not the only one who's lost the plot."

"The line about ignoring the howls is some sort of lone wolf reference," I said. "Call of the wild stuff. Howling at the moon. They're not for you. Get it? The howls aren't for you."

Everyone gave me a blank stare, and the Chief eventually motioned for me to continue.

"Ignore bared teeth, it's what they do," I said. "The wolf is just telling everyone to keep their distance. It's part of their natural instinct. Right?"

"If you say so," Josie said.

"Yeah, I'm lost too," Lacey said.

"I get it, darling," my mother said.

"Thanks, Mom."

"You've officially gone off the deep end," she deadpanned.

"Well, it had to happen eventually, right?" Josie said, laughing.

"What a bunch of philistines," I said, making a face at her. "The first two lines are talking about a wolf's natural behaviors, but that they're really not a threat to us. Don't you get that?"

"Uh, no," the Chief said.

"Not really," Detective Williams said, shaking his head. "But for the sake of the discussion, let's say I do. What does the poem have to do with anything?"

"The third line says does the money man have the guts," I said. "Peters is referring to Charles Howard. His money man."

"That one I get," Josie said. "But what's the reference to him having the guts?"

"The guts to prove to everyone that Peters wasn't actually crazy."

"Geez, thanks for clearing that up," Josie said.

"How much abuse did Peters take from other researchers and academics about his wolf research?" I said to Lacey.

"A ton," she said. "He was constantly the butt of jokes."

"So, if he got it from all sides about his work with wolves, how much crap do you think he would have gotten if he told people what he was really working on?"

"Growing human body parts," Josie said, nodding. "Okay, now I'm starting to catch up."

"Jeremy was very insecure," Lacey said. "And all the jokes and snide comments cut him deep."

"Okay, now I understand the poem," Detective Williams said. "But what does the line about having the guts mean?"

"It's a clue about where Peters hid his research. What's the one place out at Cabot Lodge you definitely need courage to explore?" I said, reaching for my bag. I removed my phone and made the call. "Hey, Rooster. Didn't think I'd get you. You're getting reception out there?"

"It's been decent the last couple of days. Congratulations. I hear she's beautiful."

"Thanks. She is."

"I'm sorry I couldn't get in today," he said. "But I'm going to swing by your place tomorrow morning if that's okay."

"Absolutely," I said. "Come early. Chef Claire is making breakfast."

"What are you having?" he said.

"Well, I can't speak for anyone else," I said. "But I'm starting with a Mimosa."

Everyone in the room laughed.

"It sounds like you're having a party over there," he said. "Did you call just to say hi, or do you need something?"

"Actually, I need you to look for something," I said.

"You got it."

"How are you and Thelonious getting along?"

"The male wolf in the first cage?"

"Yeah."

"Now that he's figured out I'm one of the people who feeds him on a regular basis, he's okay. It's not like I can get close enough to pet him, but his bark is worse than his bite."

"Told ya," I said, glancing around the room with a smug look.

"Don't gloat, darling."

"What's that?" Rooster said.

"Nothing," I said. "Have you fed them yet?"

"I was just getting ready to do that. Why?"

"Because after you feed Thelonious, I need you to look in the structure inside his cage."

"In his doghouse?"

"Yeah."

"What am I looking for?"

"You'll know as soon as you see it," I said, my neurons on fire.

"Okay, hang on. Let me grab his dinner from the fridge," Rooster said.

I put the phone on speaker and set it down on the small table attached to the bed. We heard Rooster close the fridge then the sound of his footsteps as he walked down the hall and out onto the back porch.

"Almost there," he said, heading down the steps.

"Take your time," I said, glancing over at Max who was still sound asleep against my mom's chest.

"Here you go, Thelonious," Rooster said, then we heard the soft thump of something landing on the ground. "I gave him an extra big portion just to keep him busy. Okay, let's see what we've got."

We sat quietly listening to the sound of Rooster crossing the cage. He groaned and followed it up with a string of expletives.

"Sorry about the language."

"Don't worry about it. Your back?"

"Yeah, it's pretty cramped in here. Hey, I see something."

"What is it?"

"It looks like a cubbyhole of some sort. Son of a gun."

"Did you find something?"

"Holy crap," he said. "How did you do that?"

"I study poetry in my spare time. What is it?"

"It's a briefcase. There's a laptop inside along with a thick document wrapped in plastic."

"Does it say anything on the outside?"

"Project Org 2020. Funding Round Four. Final Report," he said. "Suzy, you are officially my hero."

"Aren't you sweet. Would you mind bringing it with you tomorrow?"

"No problem. Maybe I'll even do a little light reading tonight."

"It's probably a great cure for insomnia," Josie said.

"Okay, Thelonious made very short work of his dinner. So, I'm going to get out of here just in case he's still hungry. Oh, tell Lacey I'm making dinner. It should be ready by seven."

"I'll be there," she called out.

"Great," he said. "See you when you get home."

Rooster ended the call, and I stared off at the far wall.

"Home?" Josie said, grinning at Lacey.

"It's just a figure of speech," she said, blushing.

I dug through my bag and found the business card. Then I made the call and put the phone on speaker.

"Charles Howard?" Detective Williams said.

"Yup. Hi, Charles. It's Suzy."

"Hey, I heard the news. How did everything go?"

"Great. Long, painful, but great."

"Congratulations."

"Thank you. Are you still in town?"

"Actually, I was just about to check out and hit the road."

"You might want to extend your stay another day."

"Okay," he said. "I can do that. Assuming I have a good reason."

"Oh, it's good. Can I ask you exactly what you're looking for?"

"You mean, Jeremy's research?"

"Yeah."

"Well, based on the last conversation he and I had, I'm looking for a document."

"Funding round four, final report?"

"Wow. You found it?"

"We did," I said. "He'd hidden it in one of the wolf cages."

Charles laughed.

"A total nutjob right to the end," he said eventually. "When can I pick it up?"

"Swing by the house tomorrow morning for breakfast," I said. "It'll be there."

"That's incredible news, Suzy," he said. "How did you figure out where he had it?"

"I'll tell you all about it in the morning," I said, stifling a yawn. "But right now, I need a nap."

"Sure, I understand. Thanks so much, Suzy. A whole bunch of people are going to be a lot better off because of that report."

"I guess that remains to be seen."

"You worry too much," he said.

"Only about the future of mankind," I said, then shrugged. "And all the dogs."

"I'll do my best not to disappoint you," he said. "Can I assume you're going to want a reward?"

"No," I said, then an idea popped. "But you can do me a favor."

"A favor? Sure. That's the least I can do. What do you need?"

"I need you to build us a really big fence."

"A fence? Man, I could have guessed all day and not gotten that. Okay, I'm sure that can be arranged. What should I bring to breakfast?"

"Just your checkbook."

I ended the call and yawned.

"Well played," Josie said.

"Thanks. Geez, I'm beat."

"We'll get out of your hair," the Chief said, then looked at Detective Williams. "C'mon, I'll let you buy me a drink."

"You guys should come to breakfast," I said.

"Oh, I don't know," Detective Williams said. "We don't want to intrude."

"Speak for yourself," the Chief said, then glanced at Chef Claire. "What are you making?"

"Whatever Suzy wants."

"Belgian waffles," I said. "And bacon."

"There you have it," Chef Claire said to the Chief.

"I'll be there," he said. Then he leaned over and gently kissed my forehead. "Get some rest."

"Thanks, Chief."

After they left, Josie and Chef Claire huddled close to the bed and hugged me.

"We'll be back later to pick you up," Josie said.

"I'll be ready," I said, having a hard time keeping my eyes open.

"Let's go," Chef Claire said. "I need to stop by the restaurant on the way home."

"Cool," Josie said. "Maybe I'll make myself a sandwich."

"I'd be shocked if you didn't," Chef Claire said. "See you later, Mrs. C."

"Goodbye, ladies," my mother said, staring down at her granddaughter. "Isn't she beautiful?"

"She certainly is," Chef Claire said, then paused in the doorway and looked back at me. "Why do you think Peters went to all that trouble?"

"You mean to hide his research?" I said.

"Yeah. It was a bit over the top," she said.

"Good question," I said, too tired to think about it.

"Maybe he figured out what Clarissa and Charlotte were up to," Chef Claire said with a shrug.

"Or the guy was just a total nutjob," Josie said.

"There is that," I said.

"It could have been worse," Josie said. "He could have been a muttonhead."

"Go home," I said, laughing through another yawn.

When they had left, I glanced over at my mother with a sleepy stare.

"You want me to take her, Mom?"

"No, she's fine right here. You get some sleep."

"Thanks, Mom. Well, we finally managed to get you a granddaughter, huh?"

"Yes. Well done, darling. You did good."

"Did well."

"Go to sleep," she said, raising an eyebrow at me.

I did.

I slept hard and dreamt deep.

Of a solitary wolf silhouetted against the backdrop of a full moon.

The wolf's howls reverberated around the city landscape I found myself in, and, as I stood there holding a young girl's hand, I couldn't decide if the howls signified the wolf merely announcing its presence to the world, or if they were meant as a warning.

A warning about the inexorable march of progress toward a world where people, people of means to be precise, could buy longevity and a healthier life.

Or, as if being fully cognizant of the landscape shifting under its feet, perhaps the wolf was asking if there would always be a place for him.

A safe place.

With room to roam.

Unfettered.

I glanced down when I felt a tiny hand squeeze mine.

"What's the wolf saying, Mama?"

"I'm not sure. Maybe he's just saying hello."

"That must be it," she said in a tiny voice. Then she squeezed my hand again. "Nothing gets past you, Mama."

"Thanks, Sweetie. I have my moments."